FAN W**O**MAN

Latin American Women Writers

Editors

Jean Franco,
Columbia
University

Francine
Masiello,
University
of California
at Berkeley

Tununa
Mercado

Mary Louise
Pratt,
Stanford
University

MEAN WOMAN

MINA CRUEL

by Alicia Borinsky

Translated and

with an introduction

by Cola Franzen

UNIVERSITY OF NEBRASKA PRESS: LINCOLN AND LONDON

Originally published in Spanish as *Mina Cruel*. Copyright
© Corregidor, Buenos Aires,
1989.

Portions of an earlier version
of this translation were published in *O.ARS* 6/7 (1989):
159–62; *Rampike* 7, number 1
(1990): 52–53; and *Polygraph*
number 4 (1990): 160–80.

Library of Congress Cat-
aloging in Publication Data
Borinsky, Alicia.
[Mina cruel. English] Mean
woman / by Alicia Borinsky;
translated and with an
introduction by Cola Franzen.
p. cm. – (Latin American
women writers)
ISBN 0-8032-1234-8 (cloth). –
ISBN 0-8032-6112-8 (pbk.)
I. Series.
PQ7798.12.0687M513 1993
863—dc20 92-37129 CIP

Contents

Introduction

"The generic filiation of this work matters little," writes Saúl Yurkievich about Alicia Borinsky's *Mean Woman*, "whether novel, fable, tale, or allegory. What is clear is the contagious gaiety with which this joyful account was written and destined as a gift for the reader."[1] Ester Gimbernat González calls it "a fin de siècle novel of disintegration camouflaged behind simulation, theatricalization, and the representation of sex, power, resistance, and exile."[2] The fact is, this novel, always in motion, resists being pigeonholed.

The place and time are never given, and although some clues clearly suggest Argentina during the years of the Peróns and the dictatorships that followed, many of the events could have occurred in other places as well. We hear, or overhear, the story in conversations, scraps of songs and patriotic speeches, slogans, asides, and notes addressed to us by the narrator-guide. The reader is drawn in as a participant in this adventure from the very first words: "LET'S GO IN ON TIPPY TOES: FIRST OF ALL THE MORAL."

Like some of the characters who drop out of sight only to resurface in another role or identity, the novel unfolds through a series of transformations, as if a kaleidoscope reflecting on a particular scene were turned again and again, causing the elements to tumble and make a new pattern with each twist. The shifting scenes and juxtapositions are manifested in headlines, fragments, and sections of varying lengths.

Mean Woman has some of the satisfying and familiar feel of a fairy tale.

1. Saúl Yurkievich, in a statement included in the Spanish edition of *Mina cruel,* tr. Cola Franzen (Buenos Aires: Corregidor, 1989).

2. See Ester Gimbernat González, *Aventuras del desacuerdo: Novelistas argentinas de los años ochenta* (Buenos Aires: Vergara, 1992), 301. Citations are translated from the Spanish by Cola Franzen.

Outrageous and grotesque happenings in the novel sound logical, on their own terms, of course. Borinsky has a way of keeping up with details or piling them up pop-art fashion: "false eyelashes with a soft upward curl that make the eyes look bigger and put color in even the palest of cheeks by a miracle of magnetism and suggestion," or "worn out from writing her memoirs, she would sit down . . . to have a nice cup of tea with tiny little sandwiches cut in triangles." She tells us what happened to the lions after the lion tamer ran away with the girl who lived on the roller coaster, and what Carmela did with the bucket she was carrying when she saw Francisco for the first time, felt the "cosmic tickle," and gave her great leap into the air.

The use of humor in *Mean Woman* is crucial as a way of dealing with one of the darkest periods of Argentina's history. As Francisco and Cristina plot to take power, Francisco starts "dreaming out loud about exile," because the main reason to gain power is to have the chance to go into exile later, in a civilized country. But the novel does not skirt any of the horrendous events that occurred, including kidnappings, disappearances and killings, torture, police surveillance and wiretaps, shortages of food and rampant inflation.[3]

However, this is not a testimonial document, but something more like

---

3. See the discussion of uses of humor in "Contar y cantar: Julio Cortázar y Saúl Yurkievich entrevistados por Pierre Lartigue," in Saúl Yurkievich, *A través de la trama. Sobre vanguardias literarias y otras concomitancias* (Barcelona: Muchnik Editores, 1984, pp. 108–21). The interview has been translated into English by Cola Franzen as "Saying and Singing," published in the literary magazine *O.ARS* 6/7, *Voicing*, 1989, pp. 5–14. Cortázar says, "In *Hopscotch* the scenes that are most terrible, most dramatic need humor to get by, to be acceptable. And in *Manual for Manuel* the humor is absolutely necessary to provoke the upset of the Great Conventions of society to make way for a more humane order" (p. 13).

the dissection of the psyche of a society as it somersaults and pratfalls toward disaster. Life goes on no matter what: The young grow up and willy-nilly go in search of identities, friends, pleasure, love, jobs, a future; worry about clothes, hairdos and makeup; try to get ahead, gain prestige, power, respect, and admiration. The contrast between this daily attempt at "normal" life and the reality of a repressive regime gone haywire creates much of the tension in the book, as the hilarious and the horrifying are braided and intertwined. "They lived like tiles of a Byzantine mosaic, each one trying to keep to its own color and occupation without knowing the pattern of the whole, . . . unseeing unhearing."

Sexuality plays a large part in this book. It could hardly be otherwise, since Borinsky is writing about a patriarchal society that regards women as mere helpmeets or playthings of men, an attitude heightened by Latin American machismo and carried to extremes by the dictatorships. The sexual mores of the men in *Mean Woman* can be illustrated by Francisco: "He realized that he had accomplished all the basic rites of masculine existence. He had been father, husband, employee. His orgasms, broadcast far and wide in the social sense, had granted him an identity." And then there are Francisco's muchachos,[4] young zealots who prowl the city by night looking for prey: "They are young and have the itch for action in their bones, they fuck night and day, they are making the country, making babies, making trouble."

But this novel is really about women. The title of the original in Spanish,

---

4. The general meaning of *muchachos* in contemporary usage in Spanish is simply *young men*. In Peronist jargon, it was an affectionate term that Perón used for his young supporters who were willing to do anything for him. The word reinforced Perón's paternalistic role; the Peronist march was even called "Los muchachos peronistas." Because of its specific meaning in the context of the novel, the Spanish term has been retained in *Mean Woman*.

Mina cruel, comes from the lyrics of a tango, in which the male singer bemoans the fact that his *mina* has come back to disturb his peace of mind after having abandoned him earlier. The word *mina* came from lunfardo, the underworld slang of Buenos Aires, and originally denoted a prostitute who was a *mina de oro* (gold mine) for her pimp. Now the word has been accepted into popular speech and simply means *woman*, an attractive, desirable woman, though without any pejorative overtones.[5]

The women in *Mean Woman* show more energy, imagination, and curiosity than the men in all areas, including sexual matters; the men are attempting to fulfill the expectations that society has set for them while the women are trying to elude their roles. Most are ringing changes on their identities and positions, bent on escaping from their traditional slots, finding a wider area of operation, and willing to use whatever means are at hand. Rosario says, "In this world the bed is a passport to power. I am going to eat men with knife and fork, very slowly, licking my lips." Cristina manipulates Francisco and wheedles favors from him when not "curled up like a little cotton ball between his life and the bed." Carmela stops being wife, mother, exemplary office worker. "What do I care, she said and her insides sang, whistled a selfish, exciting pleasure. . . . Let them croak— and let me dance the hokey-pokey." And there are the Friend, the SELF-MADE WOMAN, and a number of others. "One *mina* after another parades past in the first three chapters," writes González, "unknotting strings . . . that mark out the limits of predictable dependencies and crosses to bear, . . . each one choosing a different way out."[6]

Micaela appears in the second section in a "soggy double-spaced

5. See José Edmundo Clemente, "El idioma de Buenos Aires," in Jorge Luis Borges and Clemente, *El lenguaje de Buenos Aires* (Buenos Aires: Emecé Editores, 1963; reissued by Alberto J. López, Buenos Aires: Impresiones, 1984).

6. González, *Aventuras del desacuerdo*, 303.

portrait" with the warning that this is the heartwarming, sentimental part of this story, and indeed Micaela cries all the time even when she sleeps, a witty parody of the García Márquez brand of magic realism. "It was during those days that Micaela's house filled with birds and ostriches and horses and cows. From every direction they came to bathe in the puddles caused by the rain and the tears. They came out of the house tinted by the colors of Micaela's dreams who in the last twenty years had begun to dream memories in Technicolor."

Just as *Mean Woman* is rooted in an identifiable period of history, the book comes from a particular current of Latin American, particularly Argentinian, writing that began around the turn of this century. By then the great innovating currents of literature and art from Europe and North America had been absorbed and submerged in a remarkable creative surge that continues unabated to this day. Since 1945 the Nobel Prize for Literature has been awarded five times to Latin American writers. During all of this period, Argentina has been at the forefront in producing daring and exciting literary works that opened many new paths in both poetry and fiction.

The precursor and inspiring figure for Argentinian writers for generations has been Macedonio Fernández (1874–1952), about whom Alicia Borinsky has written a great deal of critical work.[7] Naomi Lindstrom, who calls Macedonio "a classic case of an innovator who was ahead of his time," points out that his followers, the writers of the Latin American

7. In addition to many articles, Alicia Borinsky's works on Macedonio include *Epistolario de Macedonio Fernández* (Buenos Aires: Editores Corregidor, 1976), *Macedonio Fernández y la teoría crítica: una evaluación* (Corregidor, 1987), and the editorship of "Macedonio Fernández," in *Museo de la Novela de la Eterna* (Buenos Aires: Centro Editor de America Latina, 1967). The English edition of *Museo,* under her general editorship, is forthcoming from the University of Pittsburgh Press as part of the Archivos series of Latin American Classics.

"new novel" (popularly known as the "boom"), had to pave the way for their master so that Macedonio's own work could be understood and accepted outside a small circle of enthusiasts. Lindstrom says, "To appreciate the new novel, readers had to master the skills needed to approach Macedonio's work. They learned to construe meanings for fragmented texts, to accept characters who were not meant to be lifelike, and to follow narrative leaps in time and space."[8]

Macedonio's inventive ideas have continued to reverberate among many writers who have come along since, including Jorge Luis Borges, an early and enthusiastic booster and follower of Macedonio, Julio Cortázar, Carlos Fuentes, Gabriel García Márquez, and Alicia Borinsky herself. Not surprisingly, Borinsky has written critical studies of most of the writers mentioned here.

Alicia Borinsky was born in Buenos Aires and grew up there, becoming part of the generation of writers that includes Luisa Valenzuela and Ricardo Piglia. Her childhood was spent in the heyday of the Perón era within a family of Eastern European exiles who had arrived in Argentina fleeing the Nazis in Poland and the pogroms in Russia. She began writing poetry while very young, and from the outset was drawn to work that sidestepped the traditional separation between genres and tended to mingle them together. Buenos Aires, with its cosmopolitanism and manifold history, holds a special fascination for Borinsky. Her long walks through the city, the *porteño* world of circus performers, nighttime café characters, tango lyrics, and political dreamers of all stripes, Latin American and European, who converged in Argentina—all have had a decisive impact on Borinsky's writing. A military coup in 1966 motivated her to leave her country and undertake literary studies in the United States. No wonder that sud-

8. Naomi Lindstrom, "Macedonio Fernández" in *Latin American Writers,* 3 vols., ed. Carlos A. Solé (New York: Charles Scribner's Sons, 1989), 2: 485.

den departures, political upheavals, and a questioning of the stability of
the self in the contemporary world appear time and again in her poetry and
fiction, including the present novel.

Borinsky is still very much a part of the literary life of Argentina, maintaining close contacts and friendships with Argentinian writers and artists
living abroad as well as in Buenos Aires, and she returns regularly for visits
with family, friends, and colleagues. She went to Buenos Aires for the
publication of *Mina cruel* and was interviewed extensively on radio. The
book has had quite an impact, particularly on the younger generation.
Because she is equally at home in several worlds—Latin America, Europe,
and North America—her work has a wide reach but is perfectly anchored.
It is deeply rooted but not provincial, cosmopolitan but not free-floating.
As has been demonstrated over and over—Joyce and Dublin, Proust and
Paris, Faulkner and Oxford, Mississippi—the most universal verities often
spring from the most secure sense of place.

In addition to an important body of critical work, Alicia Borinsky has
published two volumes of poetry, the most recent being *Mujeres tímidas y
la Venus de China* (Buenos Aires: Editores Corregidor, 1987). My translation into English, called *Timorous Women,* was published in 1992 (Peter-
borough, England: Spectacular Diseases Press). *Mean Woman* represents
her most ambitious piece of fiction to date; most of her shorter fiction
remains unpublished. Another novel is in progress, tentatively called
Sueños del seductor abandonado (Dreams of the abandoned seducer) as
well as a volume of poetry, *La pareja desmontable* (The collapsible couple).

Finally, a word about the translation of *Mean Woman*. This attempt to
capture and render into English such a volatile work has been an absorb-
ing and stimulating journey. I have enjoyed the wholehearted support and
help of the author in all phases of the process. In a slight departure from the
original Spanish and from my original translation, Alicia Borinsky has

made some revisions in the first two chapters of this edition to create a more open, less secretive, gateway.

Mean Woman is an exhilarating and original mix of fantasy-history, real-unreal, comedy-tragedy. Its oblique angles and fun-house-mirror reflections reveal all the pieces of the mosaic, leaving to the reader the pleasure of making the final arrangement.

Cola Franzen

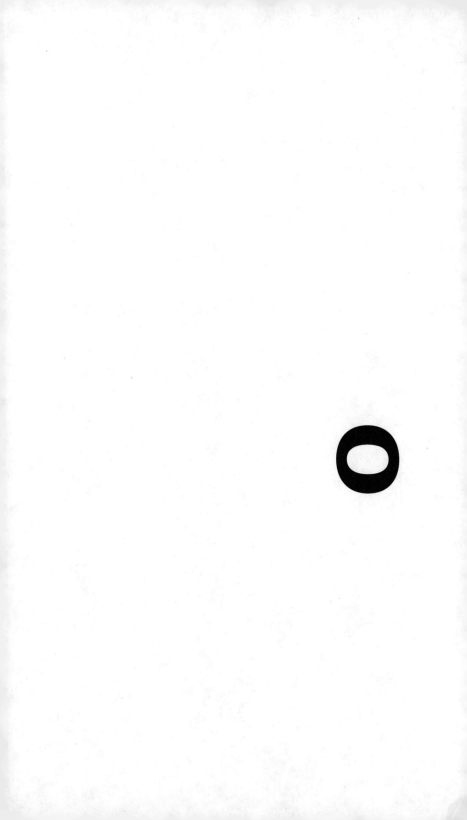

LET'S GO IN
ON TIPPY TOES:
FIRST OF ALL
THE MORAL

5

HER PREHISTORY (EVERY WOMAN HAS ONE) AND THE UNNERVING CAST OF CHARACTERS THAT FOLLOWED HER TOO CLOSE FOR COMFORT

Full face and profile she had the air of a virgin. Perfectly framed in faraway thoughts, she held on for no reason to a virtue that gently nudged her to shatter, to try and make up a symmetry of which she could only be a victim. But, dear readers, there were vexations because she would have sudden flu attacks, dizzy spells and   would get   OH   SO CONFUSED by her own excessive bookishness. Teachers, lovers, relatives shoved her to the sidelines and smiled broadly at the camera. THIS THEY WOULD SHOW THEIR CHILDREN, this pose and no other, arm in arm wearing suits, standing upright. As for her, she lingered at certain tables in an attempt to strike up bosom friendships with strangers, tried out elegant phrases to resemble movie stars, but the photographs of Theda Bara yellowed by the minute in her cramped room. That is why, my friends, she quite simply REORGANIZED, went to the corral, and there, in a low voice, started inventing wondrous state secrets, a frivolity to match her dreams.

As often happens, however, there was too much stuff, too much weight downward, toward that point they insisted on calling earth   floor   anchor.

The other characters are different. They look honest, sincere, consistent. We pay attention to them because they hold a moral. Always, always, always running counter to her story they play tricks on her, wear suits and ties, uniforms, call her mean woman but, of course, they are merely surveying everything from the cheapest, faraway seats. UNLIKE US.

TIME TO PUT ON
THE MUSIC

9

dear hometown girl/pride of the neighborhood/
one day a fluttering bird . . .

Good news. She had a part-time job. That is how she earned enough to buy paints and half the day, the most beautiful half, was made possible. Off to the port to gather up castoffs from foreign countries, to the docks to search for scraps of wood, fruit, glass, multicolored rubbish, to downtown restaurants to steal tablecloths, napkins, lace handkerchiefs thrown elegantly beneath the table, remains of heel lifts for out-of-style pumps, used condoms sweetly wafted from a window of a hotel apartment, bits of fingernails in elevators of apartment houses; the floor   the marvelous floor   the rich garbage cans   the brilliant nylon bags flying around on a windy day. To paint, re-arrange, shape, construct and from fragments, shit, the trash emerged elaborated, elegant, solid dentures. What songs and sighs as she worked. What spasms and soft tickles with every perfect smiling mouth. She loves the gaiety and gathers   gathers up any shit to turn it into teeth. Biting, biting is the best thing in life, the most beautiful song, the peak of orgasm and eating. She is a friend of Yankee and Japanese sailors who give her pieces of plastic, acrylic, scraps of Kleenex, police bulletins, round-trip tickets, deodorants. Everything to crank out sets of teeth as varied in color and texture as any meant for biting, as well adapted to gaiety and fantasy as dancing, love, the wide and toothless world. She loved her teeth and her bits and pieces so much that she was forced out of her rented room. Fucking bitch, daughter of a witch, she yelled at the landlady, grinning all the while, her enormous bags on her shoulders as she waited for a taxi that would take her to the amusement park.

You guessed. She lost her part-time job but   she earned the right to live and work on the roller coaster. In return she was to sing instead of the record player. What spectacular leaps. What a stomach brilliantly adapted to danger. The changing shifts. Her voice sounding magnificent in the middle of the park. She sang La Pera tangos, Verdi arias, gave away sets of dentures to pensive children clinging to the arm of an aunt, danced the flamenco in the air and shouted flirtatious remarks to wary Russian sailors. The day the police arrived she already had everything prepared to skip out. While the others gesticulated, explained, showed contracts and papers, she escaped with the lion tamer and a lawyer in case things got too realistic, as the lion tamer used to mutter as he arranged his neat moustache.

It was a cruel and passionate romance. She ordered him to get up early and to clean

> his lions
>
> his footsteps
>
> the traces of semen on the floor of the tent.

He showed her pictures of women caught up in their household chores and asked her to follow their example. He recommended psychoanalysts, doctors, psychiatrists, classes in cutting and sewing. She kept on singing and churning out her fabulous collection of dentures.

In the afternoons, or at night, sometimes in the morning, at dawn, you could hear the uproar, the bellows of powerful orgasms that frightened the lions and disturbed the lawyer involved in the tedium of rounding up something to eat.

AH FAMILY LIFE   NOTHING BETTER THAN FAMILY LIFE

They were happy but it had to end. The incompatibility was only too obvious. Finally the lawyer won out. With his body, his swivel hips and contracts, he managed to convince the lion tamer to leave her flat with her bags full of teeth and her orgasms. She saw them leave arm in arm, lamenting the fact that they could have no children but bent on forming a proper household, and when they were out of sight, she took matches, branches, paper, kerosene and hate, and made a fearsome fire, a cecil b de mille conflagration, burned her dentures, her bags, the documents and photos of herself when she was a star student.

Gentle, hypochondriac readers:

She also undergoes THE CHANGE and it makes us all upset, almost shivery because she blows hot and cold.

They knew her as The Pale One. Oh brother, what a puss, what a face like a horse's ass.

Dressed all in black, the neckline not even hinting at the possibility of a caress. At school they were frightened to death of her and around town the schoolgirls said that not even the sound of a mosquito was heard in her classes because she didn't say a word either. It was a battle of looks and she always came out the winner. She was professor of humiliation and obedience and was soon recognized as the undisputed mistress of the field. They invited her to conferences in Vienna, Paris, Rome, Chapultepec, Calamuchita, Arkansas, Zurich, the Canary Islands. In Las Malvinas she found her new destiny. With her exigent, sadistic, sonofabitchy glance, she electrified a brilliant female colleague who was showing promise as one of the greatest talents in the field of humiliation but was not yet so skilled in eliciting obedience. She offered to give her colleague private classes in obedience so that she might improve her curriculum, her possibilities for rising in the ranks of a discipline that was becoming more competitive every day. Delighted, delighted, thank you, thank you very much. Two women dressed in black enter an austere hotel room in Las Malvinas.

Beneath her clothes

what beautiful tattoos
what gay colors
the pulsating skin

12

the dancing round breasts

the nostalgia for the teeth

laying on of warmth and tenderness

The colleague looks and sighs, wants to try but doesn't dare but already they undress her, caress her, show her mirrors, massages, throbbing places awakened. What an afternoon that was in Las Malvinas, what joy, what fluids mingled in two hands that now reach out to one another, what a wonderful friendship, what an all-out battle against blackness, cold, humiliation.

They formed a duo of Russian singers and dancers, one called Anastasia and the other Dimitri. The Kremlin Two they were billed in the sailors' bars of Montevideo, Buenos Aires, Sweden, Baltimore. But in Cuzco they reached the zenith of glory and there they stayed for quite some time singing and dancing in Russian, without the despotism, with such gaiety that the performances ended in massive orgies, financial happiness galore, riches provided by the participating bodies. FIGHT BOREDOM WITH NAKEDNESS the poster at the entrance read, so the people who came were a plain hedonistic bunch skilled in the arts of vagrancy and caresses.

On the boat they received splendid service. Canapés with cheese and quince jelly. Stateroom with double bed. Admiring glances. No smiles when they were introduced as Anastasia and Dimitri. But the memories, the nostalgia, the hen lost in the last scandal, the way they left the show, all kept dogging their footsteps. Oh, what sadness. Sadness on top of sadness. They drank gin and fanned themselves as they looked at the sea and the twilight and alternately read Nietzsche and Cronin. Dead horses on all sides and birds that fell quicker than the whishwhoosh of a fan on a day of stiffling heat. Malarial butterflies, buzzing insects everywhere, tiny sandwiches gone suddenly green, pimples on the fingers and nails peeling off like the walls of old buildings. Dimitri died with painful rasps, trying hard not to vomit, much less in Anastasia's presence, it disgusted him to leave that image behind him, even though his last vomit was a colored, aromatic effluvium, essentially offering. It is your body, my love! shouted Anastasia grateful for the vomit, the memory.

For sanitary reasons they took away from her the little flask in which she had managed to keep the most meaningful leftovers of Dimitri's presence. They threw him into the water and disinfected her in spite of her resistance. With money collected during the confusion, under the pretext of establishing a fund to aid unemployed flamenco dancers of the Caribbean area, Anastasia arranged for the publication of a long obituary in the most important newspapers of the world announcing the death of The Kremlin Two. She spent some of the money for bribes, forged letters from readers to important weeklies, manufactured a suicide in Switzerland and was able to create a great grief, a famous burial and obscure interviews in Juliaca, Puno, Chivilcoy.

The remedy for depressions, duplications, changes of personality and toothpaste is to stop traveling. She knew it the very moment she arrived with bulging suitcases at a small village near the Peruvian border. Enough of baggage, ancestral bones, ticket stubs. She installed herself in a comfortable tent beneath a century-old tree and painted a dainty poster that said: PATRIARCH OF THE PEOPLE RECEIVES STRANGERS. EXCHANGE ADVICE AND PATIENCE FOR ANIMALS AND FOOD. It wasn't hard to get them to call her oh venerable patriarch and to believe that her singularly young and feminine face was the result of a profound process of spiritual purification that had been going on for years. "The tree and I are old and young, wise and strong." Standing with a foot propped on a rock and a hand always pointing at the exact same spot, she made speeches that became famous immediately. In general she was against the contraband of washing machines, refrigerators and electric knives that certain unscrupulous Yankee pirates smuggled over the border from Bolivia in exchange for ridiculous dark glasses with which they bribed the guards. The consequences of the contraband were numerous and all bad; the fad of dark glasses had some appalling esthetic effects. Children grew up without ever seeing their parents' faces and convinced that when they were grown their eyes would turn into glass; the movie stars who traveled incognito were constantly confused with the guards and were offered bribes that allowed them to abandon their artistic careers and swell the work force at the border; the washing machines started a cleanliness cult and the centrifugal movement suggested philosophical schools of the eternal return; water and soap were required and in periods of total drought people went so far as to wash their clothes with carbonated drinks that left them sticky and sweet, giving rise to new sexual habits, perversions and pleasures dependent on the world of the consumer, the distribution of bottled drinks, the availability of sugar, the style of the clothes. An enormous dissatisfaction became chronic in the bodies of the washingmachinemaniacs. As for the electric knives perhaps it is useless and in bad taste to speak of them at all. It is enough to say that corpses carefully cut into slices offered food for every kind of raptor which meant people could no longer hear the songs of other, more humane birds. The croaks, the clashing of beaks, the heavy wing flaps of birds with sated stomachs filled the nights of the besieged village. For this reason they became so dependent on the hermetically sealed refrigerators that pre- served the corpses at the same time they prevented gluttony; but what to do about the noise of the beaks against the doors, the voracity of the birds that threatened to do away with the living?

The foreigners would come to the tent and listen to her diatribes with a devotion born of necessity and desperation. They understood the sin of consumerism and contraband, the necessity to pay and repent, and took

15

pleasure in leaving her the fruits of their ever poorer harvests, their cows and hens. She became immensely rich and soon people forgot about her precarious arrival and began to speak of an immemorial wealth given by gods as proof of her memorable lineage. The number of her followers grew and stringent rules were adopted restricting the number of residents in the village. ONLY FOREIGNERS ARE ADMITTED IN THE SESSIONS had to be repeated over and over; more and more people poured into the areas of the village that had been deserted up to then, a complicated system of public transportation was set up, fairs and circuses were encamped a few kilometers away offering solace after her devastating speeches. The women worked as prostitutes and the men as clients, the cases in which husbands paid their own wives entered the annals of the time as an example of the indignity and inefficacy of vice. The different sins multiplied her capacity for miracles. She cured the sick, turned a pair of prostitutes into nuns, castrated the male bully of a neighboring village, solved three mathematical problems.

The mother of a child kidnapped on the way to Santiago de Compostela arrived one evening with her bag of photographs and school notebooks. Since she refused to stay *off-limits* from the village, she could not be helped. She walked to and fro showing the miraculous photographs, insisting on the miracle of a child kidnapped by god. Her persistence, good taste and capacity for work made her into a fierce competitor. Marketing techniques learned in the United States, a knowledge of bank interests studied in Switzerland and different shrewd maneuvers of erotic persuasiveness brought over to her the wide-eyed clientele of out-of-towners.

She ate her cows, hens, the tent straps and one night after surreptitiously burning her patriarch's beard, took the road to the whorehouse.

16

She spent delicious hours inventing the most curious dances and contortions for the same group that had suffered through her speeches. She wove intricate patterns of arms and legs unleashing sticky and humble fluids. Various times she repeated to herself that this was happiness and still believed it even as the electric knife sank itself amorously into her waist.

**SHE WAS NOT SO ALONE. HAD A TWIN.
HAD LOVERS.** This, dear readers, is her soggy,
double-spaced, doubly conceived portrait.
Be warned, it is also heartwarming, sentimental
and could use some uplifting.

As she knits she cries and cries until the tears soak the wool and then oh my goodness it's ruined my little yellow sweater with violet and crimson stripes that I was supposed to give to Patricia for Christmas. But she always cries and cries and balls form and the sweaters and shawls and little berets with pompoms everything is left damp balled up with ten years of wear and the sadness of a lifetime and Micaela sits and keeps on knitting and weeps and keeps on weeping asking them to leave her in peace that she doesn't need handkerchiefs or massages for her lumbago, or a nice cup of tea with a little lemon, and also she doesn't need to listen to the radio. Only silence.

There seated in the entryway streaming tears meekly every afternoon from four till seven-thirty time to leave the knitting and busy herself with more important things: clear the breakfast table and prepare it for supper, light the candles for the dead on each side of the photographs, iron the smock so the little girl can be the glory of the class tomorrow and everybody can say Micaela may be old but still so clean and so hard working because here the tears are very useful, they dampen the smock and afterwards the very hot iron leaves it shining, new, every little pleat in place.

The impeccable chignon and the girl complaining that all the young people are alike   she wants a loose one, the fitted ones are out of style and she would be ashamed   SHAME   now nobody in this world will ever feel ashamed again   Micaela knows it keeps on crying and ironing the pleats lovingly her face like a red poppy   immersed in her watery but never pathetic silence.

The only hard thing at first was to sleep without waking with a start because of the puddle that would form beside the bed and sometimes threaten to drown her when she slept more than a week straight. Micaela learned to swim while dreaming and it was beautiful to see her during one of her long torpors when for days on end she would move her arms and legs gently and harmoniously while the little girl played hookey from school, ran around with gangs of thieves and acrobats, wandered through bars, destroyed the knitted things and spent entire days dressed as a lady vamp smoking with an ivory cigarette holder.

She could do anything she wanted without arousing any suspicion at all because she fetched her twin sister from the forbidden room, sent her to school, made her go to Mass, to confession, look after the health of their aunt. When Micaela was about to wake up she hid her twin again and swallowed the key to the room only to vomit it up again on the dot every time Micaela fell asleep lachrymose on the bed with the brocade cover and the threadbare silk sheets and nylon rugs so that the floor wouldn't be ruined by so much dampness.

On her thirty-first birthday the girl decided she was through with poverty, with the mediocrity of a life devoted to swallowing and vomiting the same key, turned oily and rubbery over time; what's more the twin sister was no longer satisfied with her usual outings and also wanted to go wandering through nightclubs, make love to sailors from faraway, countries where you could only be admitted by special invitation and a sheaf of officially notarized documents. School was boring because between them the two sisters already had a diploma as a schoolteacher and instead of throwing chalk, playing hide-and-seek, red rover, hopscotch, london bridge, and stealing the solutions of problems from schoolmates, now had to teach division, multiplication, addition and subtraction of patriotic holidays, the genealogy of peacocks, the order of coleoptera, how to make and unmake cooking recipes, instruct in how to cross the street and what to do in case of an earthquake. That village was hounded by the possibility of another earthquake like the one that had brought them all to this place many years ago, so long ago that nobody could corroborate it for certain, except for one old man who had been the first to leave and who still trembled and trembled but could not speak because of what the psychologists call birth trauma. Money was raised in the village to pay for a proper treatment that might make him stop trembling and give him back the power of speech, but since an inevitable precondition was that he recall the past that was the same as everybody else's and that no one else knew either, nothing effective could be done. And all that in spite of the large and serious annual competitions that were carried out called ONE EARTHQUAKE ONE for which each inhabitant of the village posed a question and the best question won. The queries were proposed to the old man and if he didn't answer and kept on trembling, the second best and if not, the third best and so on successively until they went through all the 6,789 questions that the inhabitants of the village had posed plus those of the prisoners and the lunatics and those shut up in cages in the zoo for being indiscreet and retarded. That way the competition was very popular because everybody won. The prize was to listen to the question sung by the most beautiful woman from the neighboring village who came every year for the occasion and now getting older and so completely forgetful about her age that it had been recalculated at least ten times. She still kept the same look that had driven all the men in the madhouse crazy and for that reason the asylum had been built by the side of the plaza where the competition was held. On that date the guards allowed the windows to be opened, the men would heave great sighs, and since it was so hot, it was a blessing because a humid and amorous wind would start to blow that made flowers bloom, fields turn green and big cloud banks billow up that two days later would release a fruitful and aromatic rain.

It was during those days that Micaela's house filled with birds and ostriches and horses and cows. From every direction they came to bathe in the puddles caused by the rain and the tears. They came out of the house tinted by the colors of Micaela's dreams who in the last twenty years had begun to dream memories in Technicolor and so her tears came out the color of blue and iridescent ball gowns and often an infamous brown and then the animals fled terrified and disillusioned and prayed to heaven all together that Micaela might stop sailing and swimming in her sea of strife, intrigue, angry lovers, and would go back to remembering the light summer sweaters, christening mornings and the easter of resurrection.

The girl did not share these hopes. She only used the water to soap up her hair with her sister and to take advantage of the situation, to think that they were four who were living cheerfully hidden in rooms strewn with gumdrops, chocolates and the latest fashion magazines, particularly after the man who sold dietetic products came out of the church saying he had discovered a lotion that women could use to make themselves invincibly beautiful. All they had to do was to smooth it on their hips and the fat that accumulated on the violet sponge used for that purpose was then wiped over their breasts, which would then turn into irresistible lilting dancing flesh, roundly dancing. The men of the village didn't take to the idea. They were the type who prized the ugliness of their women intensely because it allowed them to have mistresses, go looking for love affairs in the neighboring village without having their wives complain or ask for money for clothes or lipsticks, compacts of powder or false eyelashes with a soft upward curl that make the eyes look bigger and put color in even the palest of cheeks by a miracle of magnetism and suggestion.

A fever spread among the women to cream themselves and caress each other with the sponges. Marvelous friendships developed, there were caresses they didn't know about, some began to forget about the sponges and to massage one another with their hands, pass them over the never-dreamed-of smoothness of the woman next door, and with a certain dewey and sometimes yearning wonder, they became acquainted with breasts, hips, stomachs, other vaginas.

There were conflicts but also loyalties. That period was known in the local history as the era of the feather because when the women chose their woman companion they would put ostrich feathers in their ears so as to block out the laments of the men who now found them more desirable and beautiful than their foreign loves and walked through the streets tearing up their airplane tickets for weekend round-trips breakfast included. On one of those evenings of desperation and madness and cries of newborns abandoned in the streets by mothers enamored of the body, the softness and roundness of women friends, the girl picked up a torn plane ticket from the ground.

She put it back together bit by bit, pasting the edges, reconstructing the dates. Great glee. Tickets were more expensive for women because the men were afraid they might decide to escape and take revenge on their innocent distant lovers. The girl would never have been able to buy a ticket for herself. She had not even been able to save enough during the ten years she charged an entrance fee to see Micaela swimming in her watery colored dream. Obviously not many people came to see her now because new superstitions were spreading. And the rumor went around that there were shifting mirrors in the house; it was because they had seen the girl and her twin sister in an off moment and were afraid of being duplicated themselves in those times of austerity and thin soup.

But the ticket, to dance around with the ticket, put on her false eye-lashes and rouge, clean the cigarette holder; be able to travel alone without some skinflint smuggler who won't even take you to a nightclub or a visiting millionaire who would fall for a little bat of the eyelashes. By herself in a luxurious airplane and the stewardesses with such beautiful faces that they ought to hide them behind a mask so that the men would not become furious and the women green with envy. No baggage whatsoever because at this stage the girl wanted nothing more than her little strawberry-red dress with the natural silk scarf knotted around the neck and a small Chanel-type bag with a gold chain in which to keep scads of cosmetics and also the miraculous sponge in case she should gain weight from eating so many tiny sandwiches, so many canapés of cream cheese with red pimento peppers and those olives so round and black.

MYSELF,
I'VE ALWAYS PREFERRED
A CLIMATE ON THE
DRY SIDE

AH the great voyage to the outside   far from the worn-out humid, vaguely uterine landscapes of Micaela toward a city. A place where, the easy meanders through nevernever land forgotten, she might find it amusing to be in the middle of urban life, in that businesslike atmosphere, real and politic, where her feminine compliance would find real oppressors, weapons to transform herself into another, to soak up without the aid of movies an image that little by little she would deem proper.

So, for this leg of her voyage she buried for good the memory of her twin—buried it, pushed it deep down, mingled it with her days and nights, the confused aroma of the plane, turned it into a weight, a twinge of guilt, an LP, a fog, a fear, and she swore to pay it off in installments whenever possible.

When she landed she already knew about the drought. The planes of Pan American, Braniff, Lan Chile, Iberia were carrying flags with them that could be placed on newsstands along with papers, journals, little bottles of lavender water, documents.

FRIENDS: WHAT ARE THE LIMITS OF PROFESSIONALISM?

What we have here, of course, is a professional woman. Her dedication to her own identity did not recognize the slippery limits of confusion. The past had gone through a dryer whose centrifugal movement—at every turn—had erased the minute nightmarish rales that still distracted certain bureaucrats from their work and made them gag.

She found a job tailor-made for her ambitions. In the morning she would leave her rented room in an apartment belonging to a widowed lady with a hazy interest in upholstery, and walk to the real estate agency. Alert and confident, she glowed as she carried folders to the office of the director of the company. Good morning, Sir; Good morning, Miss. Little treacly smiles, a wink of the eye and furtive trysts in the hotel on the corner during lunch hour.

She advanced slowly in her career because it was a backward country, finished as far as the future was concerned, carefully preserving the privileges of the past for a group of melancholy but ferocious landowners. Her greatest successes were in the field of comprehension and patience, and her talent for versatility was truly admirable. For years she tuned her body like a radio: avid midday lover for the boss and stubborn nighttime virgin for an office mate sweetheart whose fingernails were chronically black from carbon paper.

When the moment came to get married, everyone admired her composure. The parents of her fiancé congratulated themselves for her lack of passion that bespoke a long and fortunate marriage. In the small apartment they rented on the outskirts of the city, she aged slowly, without realizing it. It must have happened while she was taking her children to school or discussing the price of meat with the butcher.

She no longer needed the erotic vanities of the boss. Her moment of relaxation was centered on the dial of the TV set. During the siesta, marvelous soap operas carried her away to a territory of conflicts, electrifying events whose major virtue was that they were remote. Screw the others, she sang within herself. What do I care, she said and her insides sang, whistled a selfish, exciting pleasure. She gave up being mother, former office worker, wife,—let them croak—and let me dance the hokey-pokey, I shit on them.

What wails when her slippers were discovered under the bed without her feet, her blouse without her body, the meals not made, the clothes dirty. There was never a more perfect woman nor an office worker more dedicated to her tasks.

They never found her but they searched for her diligently until they located a substitute, one a little younger, more up-to-date, since she was able to convince the father, now her husband, to wash his hands with acetone to remove the ink from beneath his nails. Of course she too might leave but now the family didn't worry about it because they had found the ideal agency, which could provide expert professional women with talents for any task fitting for their fair sex.

ONE AT A TIME, PLEASE

33

COME IN WITHOUT MAKING NOISE   WIPE YOUR FEET ON THE MAT
READ THE REGULATIONS BEFORE ASKING A QUESTION

It was a pleasant existence, with neither frictions nor unexpected thrills. In the afternoons she went for walks in the park and amused herself by feeding the pigeons. The gray courthouse personnel consisted of political appointees who spent most of their time talking on the telephone and zealous clerks who had obtained their posts after passing incredibly difficult exams and tests of patience. Cleaning the building didn't take much time and afterward she wandered through the corridors, bucket in hand, imagining fortuitous encounters with the crowds of people jostling each other in front of the windows waiting for a case to be resolved that would not even be heard for twenty years.

People slept in front of the doors of the neo-colonial building, beside a column, their stamped papers stashed in their underclothes, afraid of losing their place in line. In that country you couldn't go anywhere without first going through the courthouse. Deaths and births had no effect on the bland, bureaucratic army that floated overhead, indifferent, high above the problems of their indignant clients.

Every time they called the police, she felt something like a memory piercing her chest, something like an affliction in sympathy with those who were growing old without ever having managed to find their birth certificate, the change of address, the report card proving they had completed elementary school, any one of the infinite pieces of paper required in order to move, travel, sell, buy.

But at bottom it was all the same to her. An apathetic dance. A carnival with no drama. An existence suspended in the void unaware that one might fall.

UNTIL HE ARRIVED.

34

He forgot to wipe his muddy shoes on the mat and started asking questions without first reading the regulations. While standing in line he began singing an aria and when one of the political hacks threatened him with a life term in prison, he bellowed in a brutally wanton way, as carefree as an animal. She felt a sudden itching in her feet, a cosmic tickle, and, flinging the bucket aside, leapt high into the air, a veritable levitation that left everybody open-mouthed, including Him.

**WE WILL DO
WHATEVER NEEDS
TO BE DONE**

A truly revolutionary atmosphere. Here we have a charismatic man who sings opera, and a humble, hard-working woman giving an example of excess to a multitude tired of so many injustices.

There's no point in telling you that it was bloody, long, full of sentimental episodes of great moral uplift.

She wore clothes of the best European designers and at the same time was queen of the poor. He sang until he lost his voice, was betrayed by his supporters and betrayed those who put their trust in him. The events devastated an order, produced books of history eventually burned and not a single child was born of that political matrimony, that heroic alliance.

HOW THEY DANCE
HOW MUCH THEY GAVE YOU
WHERE DOES THEIR APPEAL COME FROM

It's the muchachos who come in search of her, they are going to beatify her, elevate her to the level of national heroine, show her to their mamas so they will die of envy.

HOW THEY LOVE ONE ANOTHER IN THEIR GYRATIONS A GO GO
HOW THEY GAZE AND LISTEN TO ONE ANOTHER AND BECOME AROUSED
HOW MOVING THE ENTHUSIASM FOR A WOMAN
HOW THEY IMITATE HER AND HOW CREATIVE THEY ARE
THEY ARE HER MUCHACHOS AND IT IS HER MOVEMENT
IT IS THE REVOLUTION COUNTERMARCHING

At this very moment they are making the icons, the slogans must be made now that there's nothing left to do. They know her and therefore they will use her until her last small breath, until the last humble little feather of her green hat.

38

Among all her names they chose to call her GREAT LADY. They suffer from an intense case of necrophilia. They want her to have her shroud made, to dress always in white to impress the crowds, make them pay taxes, work harder, provide more income for the Nation.

Machiavellian swindlers, machiavellian shitheads, she sang out from the balcony speaking by herself to the crowds for the first time and she also said that

> they had been basely deceived
>
> they had been robbed of their wages
>
> their sons had been killed

their houses sacked and their factories and their dreams and their bread made bitter and their summer games changed and the flights of birds cancelled and broadcasts of news from abroad eliminated and time stopped so that everything would be a curtain of smoke, a mere stage set for the wild dance of the greedy muchachos, bullyboys, punk revolutionaries with no feelings of generosity or love that they promised so many times but that came out like a serpent from the black leather trousers, vomit of obscene letters

> SHE TOLD THEM
>
> SHE SHOUTED IT TO THEM
>
> SHE WROTE IT IN THE SKY WITH AN AIRPLANE
>
> SHE SENT THEM LETTERS
>
> SHE PUBLISHED IT IN THE NEWSPAPERS

but they didn't believe her. They applauded her speech, went home weeping from emotion, saw it as one more proof of her love for the muchachos, a patriotic act requiring yet another sacrifice, a subtle form of

39

fidelity whose details they would have to divine in the future. The muchachos saw themselves growing stronger in the fabrication of the myth of the
GREAT LADY and they begged her to speak, to harangue the multitudes
now intent on unraveling the mysteries of her face, the meanders of her
opinions.

TAKING CHARGE

43

Her existence was so very intense that her husband died, expired because now nobody needed his operas. She was a solipsistic device for denouncing. From political themes she went on to others more intimate. There was an artistic flowering in the country thanks to her ragings and now she herself enjoyed it.

ICON AND SAVAGE, SHE REVEALS ALL

The country exported the scandal of its own existence, the harshness and richness of a tradition on the move. Small matter that such success might rest on general disbelief, small matter that the information might be in the form of words circling around them without going anywhere, like insects around a light.

ALL IS REVEALED AND ALL IS PERMITTED

It serves no purpose to talk of the emulatory customs that were founded nor of the confessional fever that pushed sinners to describe their crimes before committing them because this is the portrait of her, whose novelistic abnegation sweeps her into assuming multiform shapes, everybody's acquiescent sweetheart, cute little girlfriend.

She fled, like she always fled, full of shame but this time everything was going to have a definite end, a line with a true beginning, death and gladness in the middle. Among some old papers she found her birth certificate and as she read the names, the details, the year next to her name, her feeling of unease dissipated and she now knew the contours of a map that propelled her to another way of life and her true manner of existence.

Project became plan. She cut out her speeches and decided to smash her icon so that she could breathe, free and with all her papers, on the way to her roots.

LIVES OF SAINTLY WOMEN

In the tree a bird. Hanging on the line, clean clothes, gray pants, snowy undershirts, worn undergarments. Like an insult, a shout, a short black nylon nightie, daring and alone, waves back and forth, dry already.

Who allowed her to come in? Who gave her the key to the door, the wink and the nod so that she could addle us with her perfumes, her long long curly hair, her uncertain age?

Among the saintly women she is merely a pious charitable project. Because what she is missing is the same thing she has too much of. Because she needs what she already has, because she should be subtracted

LOSE ENERGY

LET HERSELF GO

STOP SWIMMING AGAINST THE STREAM

They had told her all this from the beginning, they had repeated it to her over and over and made her sign at the bottom of the page, here where the cross is, but she persists in trifles, in gestures of enemy efficacy that carry her far from saintliness, toward a territory of spangles, desires and memories not yet crystalized.

HER SPEECHES

I want to be like all of you. I want to ignore men, wash their clothes, serve them their meals, clean their asses with French lace hankies, care for their children, smile without hatred. Dear sisters, I want to be mechanical and lover like you, sing the praises of marriage, lovingly nurse my mops and brooms so that everything will be left gleaming.

I LOVE IT   DESIRE IT AND REQUIRE IT FROM THE BOTTOM OF MY HEART

Of course they encouraged her, patted her on the shoulder and put more lemon in the tea so that her palate would become accustomed to making subtle sacrifices. Of course they offered her companionship, but at night when the initiates got together to discuss community affairs, they whispered on and on about her case.

—Have you noticed her enthusiasm when she talks, her choice of words and her evident passion for this life?

—She doesn't see beyond the present moment. Even her blood has loud colors. She sees herself as a heroine. She wants to be a diva as well as a saint. It's pure showboating.

—I see that she despises us. She says that she prefers us but she doesn't know the meaning of friendship. She could never go day after day simply waiting for a request for help, dreaming up sandwiches for lunch, planning the exact moment to buy the most efficient and economical brand of detergent.

—Her devotion is of no use to us.

—What a misfit in her nightgown.

And Carmela went on with her chores. Making beds. Learning the voluptuous language of starched sheets. Mastering the art of folding shirts. Singing while the stew simmered on the stove. On fire with patience. When she sang, her voice took on the shape of the black nightie floating in the wind, competed with butterflies, mingled with the bellows of animals in heat.

Then came the test of her fidelity. They admitted a serious hardworking man so that he could court her. They put no restrictions on him, his decency was plain to see because there were no signs of perspiration under his arms. Francisco would arrive at dusk after a day's work and sit with her on the veranda. Carmela would ask him about his day, discretely, aware that it wasn't necessary to listen to his reply, knowing all too well that the main thing was to stay seated there until they could each learn their respective roles letter perfect.

Ah, the pleasures of cold sweethearts. Ah, stagnant blood that keeps flowing without ever racing, the heart beating like a metronome.

Dear readers of novels:

There's no need for me to dwell on what we know already. Only the most banal signs of their unequal destinies surfaced, showing the duplicity of her saintliness: a divorce trial attended by the true saints, all dressed in severe clothes, surrounded by their children and husbands. Carmela discovered that the smell of saintliness lingering between her legs after so many years of matrimony disappeared with aerobic exercises. Like so many other women wishing to erase the signs of an earlier life, she began an endless regimen that took her from water fountain for eight glasses of water daily to shower to the business of selling athletic equipment.

WHO TOLD YOU
THAT MEN ARE NOT
FICKLE?

When Francisco closed the door of his new place, he felt a pang, a new tenderness invading him. He realized that he had accomplished all the basic rites of masculine existence. He had been father, husband, employee. His orgasms, broadcast far and wide in the social sense, had granted him an identity. At forty-five years of age he found himself in good and vigorous health, moustache growing, nails with good color, and his judicious marriage to Carmela had put them both in the middle class.

Francisco burned his little black book, forgot the birthdays of all his relatives, near and distant, and lying in bed embarked on a slow masturbation that led him, with panting and perversity, along a novel path throughout a hot week. Modest pretexts of pleasure paraded through his hands and the rest of his body: the woman next door with the opulent breasts, the milkman with the wide leather girdle from which he made change, his own knees, so round, a late afternoon in the house of his maiden aunts. With hindsight, Francisco celebrated his existence, recognized himself narcissus-like, re-possessed himself with fervor.

While Carmela was in the aerobic classes swaying back and forth, jumping up and down and in and out of the shower, Josefina, unable to shed her saintliness, was eyeing her jealously.

—Are we friends or not? What good did it do me all the times I lent you my shampoo, handed you the soap in the shower? Invite me to your house, I want to eat your cooking, know your favorite corners, gossip with you about sweaters, shopping, bargains in the fancy boutiques. I want to be your special friend, lunch with you on green salad and rye bread; joke about our ex-husbands, sip mineral water. Why this rejection? Where is the invitation that never comes?

—Francisco, don't let me, don't allow me to go out like this without a new knit top or a fur wrap without even shoes with the new Parisian heels. Francisco, don't make me feel poor, neglected, ugly, alone among the wives of the other politicians, ridiculous among the lovers of the big shots.

That's what Cristina would say to Francisco when she wasn't cuddling with him or curled up like a little cotton ball between his life and the bed. Evasive and vacuous, Cristina had the power of invoking Francisco's virility by simply batting her eyes. The soldiers under his command admired him all the more when he reviewed the troops accompanied by his mistress. She showed off body-hugging clothes, chose materials that clung daringly to her curves suggesting nights of abandon in the arms of the general.

She was a banner.

She was a little masterpiece.

She was practically an entire showcase of erotic products all by herself.

Francisco had found her at the end of his long masturbation and with her came success, recognition of the weak, of those taken up with family life, children, boring jobs. Cristina inspired him to make patriotic speeches, aroused him with her lighthearted nonsense and now as an adjunct to his thirst for power, Francisco started dreaming out loud about exile.

DREAMS OF GLORY

They will come to England. All dressed up, they will come to see me bringing important papers to be left in my care, scripts for television serials, views of the tropics so that the sense of the universal will not lead me astray. They will see me living in a fabulously luxurious house paid for by their own sweat, one they will build for me far from their country so that I may preside over their dreams and mediate their disputes. They will arrive in England ashamed of not knowing the language, aware of my wisdom and my generosity and their eyes will cloud over with tears, they will get ulcers, my poor poor comrades, my beloved people, seeing me in England.

Francisco was preparing himself for exile by amassing power, intrigues, influences. Cristina purred on and on with her accountants about the national spirit while telexing money from her own computer to various banks in Switzerland and Japan.

SHOPPING AND LOVE

LET'S GO SHOPPING, LOVE, because we are getting dowdy.

Ah, the world of Cristina. Always quick to catch the newest fad of the dressmakers, always with an ear cocked so that the photographers and designers might prepare her for that prolonged bedding down with a yearning public, anxious to give power to Francisco, grateful for her beauty, bewildered by her short visits.

LET'S GO SHOPPING. WE ARE GOING TO DO A LITTLE INTERNATIONAL SHOPPING

She went to patriotic celebrations disguised as a coya, better yet, dressed as an Incan princess, imitating Ninochtka and how they applauded her, how they were aroused by her hips. What do you mean, gymnastics? You can bet your ass that's not it. That body, that swish, comes from somewhere else, from love well made, from the virile and well-tempered blood of the General.

PLEASE, A LITTLE DISCRETION

Father Gabriel received everyone in the confessional. He was the only priest left to hear them since the saintly women had caused the others to go deaf with their stubborn confessions of exaggerated and fabricated sins, problems of too much bleach and too little flagellation.

Father Gabriel never said a word to anybody. The moment he ended his nine hours of bending his ear he went to his room and there, as every night, began to fit together the details.

The filthy curses of doña Belarmina versus gorging on turkey at the wedding celebration of don Mariano's daughter Ana Alejandra.

The theft of little Cristina's pencil sharpener by the second grade teacher balanced against the lie about Lucía's pregnancy.

The pats on the ass of the secretary of the orphanage in contrast to the fake smile of the baker's wife as she greeted every single morning for the last six years the man with whose wife she carried on a daring and silent idyll.

The details piled up and repeated themselves but Father Gabriel did not give up the task of arranging his checkerboard and every night, engrossed in his game of little slips of paper, he fabricated contests from which certain sins came out victorious, thanks, for example, to the fact that someone had smiled WITHOUT MALICE or because a throw of the dice had caused THE ALL-FORGIVING ONE to appear. For Father Gabriel WITHOUT MALICE had become a sort of guardian angel and when its presence was invoked, few realized that the Father was referring to something more tangible than expressionless eyes, an innocent touch.

WITHOUT MALICE Father Gabriel whispered into Carmela's ear and only she knew that the moment had come to light the candles in the church and fly to the little Father's room to make the bodily ablutions, the spiritual exercises that would earn her the generosity of the ALL-FORGIVING ONE.

By the time night came, Carmela, worn out by the rock and roll of the aerobic exercises, was a sprightly but tired version of her attempt at saintliness. Father Gabriel's body, squishy and wrinkled, his gurgles like a baby beguiled by the outside world seemed to her like a bedraggled pillow where she could rest, round and rosy, from motion, mirrors, orders to jump higher, faster, bathe more efficiently, slim down, slim down, repeat.

Dear friends, her saintly life thus reached height and perfection, she became muddled and forgot about underclothes, her self-flagellation during the slow rales of pleasure became rarified and enfolded in order to return in another form, perhaps wearing a wig.

Don't think for a minute that Cristina didn't lead a sacrificial and spiritual life. Through Francisco she came into contact with Carmela. She understood the slightest sensations, the touches, the tastes that had shaped the lack of warmth of the first couple and without knowing Carmela's name or ever having talked to her, Cristina understood her to the core, wore her like her own underclothes, used her as her subconscious in the inevitable sessions of psychoanalysis that those in the upper levels of power were obliged to go through to give an example of introspection to a populace distracted by the fact that their salaries had not gone up.

Cristina was passionately attached to her clothes and as she undressed, she went into a trance; vanished and was dismantled and diffused into other presences. Evolved into amoeba, or Carmela, the cleaning woman, a female colleague seen by chance. What others imagined was an extraordinary body was pure panic. Cristina scratched herself in order to recognize her essence in the red blood that flowed from her wounds. She laughed and cried to plumb her own depths. Clothes christened her over and over with their price tags, colors, hints of stories.

She adored the enormous armoires that Francisco had ordered sent especially from England. Better to be prepared for exile. They will load the armoires directly on the boat and we will depart happy and well furnished. She would often crawl inside, curl up, and with hems grazing her cheeks sing military marches until she fell asleep.

Naturally at the beginning of their marriage Francisco would search for her, to consume and to consummate as he said jokingly to a detective hired to find her. But it happened that one night while looking for his slippers, he saw her hanging in the closet looking like a rag merchant and realized that she had turned into the most precious secret of his future exile.

He called her his Dolly, sweet little Valentine and the soldiers, delighted, dreamed of the General's nights, drank and sang to keep them company. Beautiful broad. What a boon for the country that cleavage. What national pride.

EVERYDAY LIFE

TRAITOR   SON OF A BITCH   PEDDLER   that's what they yelled at old Simon in the streets. With his white cane inlaid with silver he walked slowly waggling his ass slightly like someone making fun, like someone saying fuck off you. He had been roly-poly as a baby and now, at seventy-five years of age, his baby fat had settled in his cheeks and his fingers, around his eyes, making his assailants even more savage, skinny obstreperous gang that harassed him every Sunday when Simon started out for Patricia's house carrying a box of cookies by the string in one hand and his cane in the other, on his way to play a few hands of poker and eat French pastries. BASTARD MURDERER ENEMY OF THE PEOPLE   FAT PIG   BETRAYER. Old Simon's smile grew a bit wider, the fragrance of his cologne became more intense and the sparrows seemed to fly over him compassionately and expectantly.

MAY THE BEST MAN WIN

And what have you done to them, Simon? What cause have you given them to make them fuck you over so much as you start on your pleasant outings? If they don't like your televison programs, don't look at them, don't invite the neighbors in to watch you at the apex of power hurling clever bits of wisdom from the antennas; don't organize dangerous and mass demonstrations to refute you that only create more publicity for your broadcasts; don't whistle the jingles, don't adopt the styles worn by your female announcers, who, with a little peck on the cheek, muddle the return of the mini with the foundation of the banners of national pride.

Sure, old Simon. You are right, on Sundays you have to forget everything and concentrate on what really matters, little pastries of mille-feuille, the delight of cream puffs in the mouth and the cosy bulge of the wallet in the pocket.

Who are these brutes? Who are these beasts throwing rocks at you now? What makes them want to pick a fight, fall on a poor old man who only entertains the crowds with the fantasy of a country on the move? Is this, perhaps, death? A sudden halt of traffic in a street of a somewhat seedy neighborhood, a body that falls and others that strike it, hands searching, eagerly, money in the pocket?

HEY LOOK, GUYS, THE OLD MAN IS OURS.

You move slowly and give them a hard stare. What a business. How little sense of humor. Hours will pass before someone picks up the phone, calls an ambulance and they carry you away, your face covered, through the neighborhoods of this city that now does not know you. Dead and forgotten, Simon. Nobody is going to miss you. One more. Make sure the muchachos don't see you, that they don't manage to penetrate the mystery, that it not even occur to them to ask because the others will come later to fill out the forms, to search for a guilty party for filing court charges. Don't let the kids know anything or even talk about it among themselves.

This is life and this is the city. Like a lamp put out, so with your eyes, love. You saw nothing, you heard nothing. Everything happened without our having any part in it because we were so caught up in our own affairs, because the day is so short compared to what they offer us to justify it. We saw nothing, heard nothing. We will say nothing. Who remembers about the television programs, who cares about the street gangs, after all it was only Simon, old, reactionary and Jew. Nobody knows anything. That's the way we are but of course we would always immediately report any strange happening whatsoever, any break in the rhythm, the pulse of our beloved city.

This ball will not be the last but there is so much to celebrate. Cristina's birthday sums up every moment of happiness for Francisco. They pose for the photographers, the cooks invent traditional dishes and whisper the legends of his origins into the ears of newly slimmed down incredibly powerful weighty wives of generals, the virgins are prepared for their after-dinner struggles with lubricious budding beaus from Catholic schools. The entire nation awaits the birthday of the beauty, the climber who instructs everybody on how to reach the top.

—Don't go my treasure, they'll kill you. Don't pretend to be Cinderella and don't believe that Francisco is going to give you the time of day. He is head over heels in love. Cristina can do anything she wants with him. Your legs or your flattery will get you nowhere with him. You will never manage to convince him in spite of your youth. Theirs is a match made in heaven, bound by convenience. Don't you understand, Cristina will tear you to pieces when she finds out. Because she will find out and that day all your plans will go to the devil my dear daughter, sweetness of your mama's life, my Rosarito.

—Stop giving me advice, you are just an embittered old woman who doesn't understand how clever I am, my great plans for the future of this country. Of course I will dethrone Cristina. Francisco is like all men, the moment he knows I am available, he'll be off and running, our liaison will begin and his politics will only be a little smokescreen for his existence as well-serviced male. I can give the country what it deserves, organize it according to my ideas, follow the designs that destiny has imposed on me.

Mommy, mommy, mommy, stop worrying about me and keep curling my hair because I want to be the prettiest girl at the party. In this world the bed is a passport to power. I am going to eat men with knife and fork, very slowly, licking my lips; fix my curls mommy because I want to be ready, all dressed up, full of courage and irresistible.

FAREWELL RITES

They identifed old Simon at the police station, gave him a number and put his body in a nylon bag. Now what'll we do muchachos? Have to call the General, tell him what happened because he will find out one way or another, there is no telephone left untapped, no eyes or ears that can't be bought.

Call the General, let him know so he can tell us how to act every morning since the death of the old goat, what to say to the reporters, what sort of face to put on and what tale to spin for the cameras. Call the General so that we can concoct a story. He will give us vacations, reward us for our efforts, let's call the General on the purple telephone, cover our asses on this one, make it clear that we belong to the corps of the faithful. I'll call him. I'll tell him. I will take the responsibility, we have to do it now because the old goat is starting to rot, shitty Jew, the fatter they are the more they stink, who knows how much he robbed from us, and as for me I realize that he was one of ours. The bundle he must have robbed, the things we can blame on him. The phone's ringing. It's ringing and now he answers.

—You take him out of that nylon bag you dumb pricks you assholes and you throw him in the river, yes, you heard right, in the river like any other joe and nothing at all has happened here, you have not seen or heard a thing. Destroy all the papers, memos and files having to do with the case, why in hell do you write so much; take a stiff drink and don't get queasy, off to the river this minute.

The birthday party was in full swing. Cristina was laughing with her tinkling effeminate canary voice; everybody was admiring the perfect half-moon of her nails, her dress and her hairdo, she was a beauty decked out in the latest style. While the orchestra kept playing the most boring patriotic songs that everybody pretended to adore, the men compared their stripes and ribbons and waited for the chance to do each other in and the women fanned themselves and secretly looked down their noses at their best friends.

—Attention, attention. Ladies and gentlemen, the live and direct television broadcast of the birthday party of the lady of ladies, the most revered Cristina will not be hosted today by our dear friend and colleague Simon Teitelbaum. The generosity of our lady has reached don Simon also, on the occasion of this birthday, he has been sent by the government to his birthplace, in far-off Minsk, to fulfill an old dream of his. Taking advantage of this splendid present, this opportunity, the executive branch of the government wishes all people to participate in the joy of this date. Cheers, cheers and happy voyage don Simon Teitelbaum and our greetings to all immigrants who have contributed to the building of our generous country with their efforts. And now we return to the presidential mansion and to the festivities with our host Pepe San Roman.

Skinny Cristina wept and trembled beneath her ball gown. What could have happened to old Simon? How could it be that nobody had told her anything, who had gone too far with that old miracle man, her adviser, her dear dear friend, her European connection, her security that in exile she would have a guide, someone to teach her how to consort with English and Dutch women and all those civilized people so different from this country of ignorant pricks as the old man used to say. People with no taste, no culture, my dear Cristina, that's why they watch my programs, that's why they keep searching for more and more photographs of you wearing this little dress or that little hat, they don't understand and never will, they are so many guttersnipes, everyone of them, my dear, but in exile it will be different and of course that will happen because let's be frank: with all due respect, do you believe that the General can last much longer? The army is keeping an eye on him, the navy and the air force are already itching for a coup, it will come my dear and the General knows it and that's why he is filling his coffers and depositing his money in banks on the outside, the General knows and in exile my dear, what parties and what superior people, what contacts and invitations; I will put us in the jet set while the General keeps on with his politics. You have to read many novels, my dear, and you have to forget about these animals, Cristina. In exile, people of your level. Have another cookie.

How agitated the dictator's bag-of-bones wife felt beneath her party clothes, how she wanted to raise merry hell and kill off the gangs because for sure it was who it always was, Francisco's muchachos, the General's pets, with their grandstanding and foul mouths. Stupid mother fuckers, Cristina said to herself while smiling for the cameras. They are going to pay me for this. This they will pay me back in full, snot-nosed sons of bitches, snatch my special friend, my confidant, this is different, you will pay me for this one, for every single last kilo of fat Teitelbaum they will pay me, damned pricks.

Could she have been invited that girl who arrived alone in the purple dress? Who is she and why did she walk straight to the General's table? What did she say in his ear and why did they make room for her to sit down?

Cristina went looking for vengeance after the birthday party. Emboldened by her presents, the little winks the General had given her in the middle of political meetings, she felt invincible. Now to kill off the assassins of don Simon Teitelbaum. Let them also go to Minsk, let them also disappear and go floating down the river, let the good times of the muchachos be over and done with, those young bulls of the neighborhoods, stuffing themselves with juicy steaks. Serve them up to me on a platter. Yes, yes, all of you, I promise you paid vacations, a little farm in the south; no, not a word to the General don't let him know because he is very absorbed with the matter of his health, you understand.

THE MAN OF OUR DREAMS

—And as for me ever since I was a little girl I adored collecting photographs of you. At night I would take them to bed with me, put out the light and imagine that you would come close and very very slowly lift up my nightgown, I could feel your uniform grazing my skin, the tinkle of your medals over my little tits and later, well, I won't tell any more because it's too embarrassing.

—No, no, tell me, since you were a little kid you did that? And how was it you said yesterday your cunt would get all wet? Since you were a little kid? with my picture? come on keep talking while I unzip my fly, keep talking precious, little treasure, sweet slut.

Every afternoon Rosario appeared in the General's office with a briefcase full of papers and once they were alone started in once more on her prolonged seduction of Francisco. By then, after so many speeches, so many official papers and memoranda, he had almost forgotten he had a body. He took out photographs of himself in uniform and Rosario's voice awakened lubricious occasions of previous lives, invited him to love himself in the photographs, carried him to ecstasy; conjured up a nymphet lover for the General; he saw himself in bed clutching his own image, grew hot with the metallic clank of his medals.

Rosario remained unmoved by the bellows he let out when he made himself come or by the smacking of his lips or the rediscovered vigor of his semen, growing stronger as the sessions went along.

She kept the tone of her voice serious and complicitous, gave him half-smiles and added some new detail or other each time she told the story. Francisco became more and more dependent on his sticky sessions; come on, baby, tell me more about when you were little, go ahead, tell me. Why come only at three? Then stay longer than an hour, tell me again, now about your aunt who came in and discovered you and you got her in the bed with you and you did everything you could imagine while thinking of the General. Come on, tell me again; yes tell how you do it blow by blow.

In cabinet meetings Francisco seemed different, distracted and his hand never strayed far from his fly. Rumors spread about a prostate operation, that the General was on his last legs, that he shut himself up in his office every afternoon and one could hear moaning, that he didn't even seem able to work with Rosario his secretary without complaining like an animal in pain, that Rosario was the one really in charge of things, that Simon Teitelbaum had not gone to Minsk but was in Europe investigating cures for the General's pecker, that Cristina sent squadrons to kill muchachos because it had been so long since anybody had showed her what a real man could do, that in the presidential mansion nobody read the newspapers anymore for fear of scientific news that might demoralize the General.

One day Father Gabriel, returning from his evening walk, saw the fat finger of Simon Teitelbaum sticking out of the dirty water of the river and his heart turned over in his chest. He too had been chosen for something special, at last an opportunity, an achievement, a possession, his own secret, at last something different from the puny problems, petty concerns that went in one ear and out the other.

His own secret

His very own corpse

His cadaver hook line and sinker

His simple

    entire

    complete

    political dowry

Making sure that nobody was watching what he was doing, spying here and spying there, on tippy toes and laughing inside, he hiked up his cassock and started pulling on the fat finger. Bitching thing it's heavy. But anticipating luxuries and pleasures to come gave him strength and soon he was in possession of all of fat Teitelbaum.

Face to face, in his little room. Fat Teitelbaum, bloated and almost decomposed, kept sliding out of the chair so Father Gabriel had to lay him down while he made a bed of ice for him in one of the boxes kept for burying paupers. There he would spend his eternity.

Rosario, miss Rosario please hear us, please a little attention for this terrible, unheard of, out of control problem that is driving us crazy and upsetting us so much; please look at me and listen to me with your usual compassion, you who take care of us, you who are the most beautiful and upright young lady that the country has ever had, the best secretary, the pride of a line of people who are vanishing little by little; miss, miss, we have so much to tell you both individually and as a group. We don't like Cristina any more either all skin and bones so caught up in her games with the muchachos. We believe everything people say about her and that's why we repeat it, miss Rosario, because she is the one guilty of all these disappearances of the young bulls in all the neighborhoods; it's her fault that their mothers and sweethearts are suffering; she got her clutches into them with those innocent kids and so what if they feel like beating up somebody now and then and so what if they don't give a shit about foreigners and so what if they don't like jews. They are young and have the itch for action in their bones, they fuck night and day, they are making the country, making babies, making trouble. Miss, miss we also don't think the General loves Cristina any more, you should know, you who have no quarrel with the muchachos, you who shit on all the stories of Teitelbaum and Minsk. Listen to us miss and you will see that we will all come out winners. One of these days we will carry her out on a stretcher and there will be no more secrets. One of these days we will put Cristina in jail, give her what she deserves, break the spell of her power. Oh, miss, listen to us.

So Rosarito dreamed on and plotted every night in her bed in the rooming house next door to the presidential mansion. She puffed herself up proud as a peacock but in the morning, when the damp air of the city weighed down reminding her of the truth of her life, she told herself that every session with Francisco was bringing her closer and closer to her objectives. But Francisco, in love with his photographs and the stories of the little girl aroused by the General, soon realized that he needed something more substantial than the bland sessions of masturbation. After all, why be content with that little girl voice? Why not go on to the act itself like a man of action, a real he-man of a country on the move?

Dressed as a girl, Francisco sighed and reveled in the pleasures of the body of his chauffeur, an astonished tubby man from the provinces who soon learned to handle the General's uniform very effectively, using the tinkle of the medals and the force of his erect member to satisfy his boss's militaristic schoolgirl longings.

They began to tell Rosario that the General wasn't in, that he had important affairs to take care of that day, that perhaps it would be better not to come back or that she should make an appointment with Madame Cristina if it was something really urgent, and who had allowed her access to this room, that in any case she should file all the documents necessary for her petition and through the mediation of some lawyers she might be granted a hearing. Rosario saw the scenario of her rainbow evaporate. She didn't understand it because at bottom she was just a simple neighborhood kid and the true passions of men were mysteries to her. She gradually fell into a deep sadness. Stopped curling her hair.

Decided her mother was right.

Went back home.

Got a job as cashier in a store.

Taught in an elementary school.

Became a nun.

REVENGE AND OBLIVION

Cristina's campaigns were very bloody, the depth of her resentment ravaged the country and there was no corner that couldn't count a few deaths to remember the fury of the lady who would send her henchmen out at night to strike seemingly at random. After many months, the disappearance of fat Teitelbaum lost its bite, ceased to weigh on her heart because by then she knew she had turned the entire country into a wailing morass. Only then could she sit down to pack her bags and at last arrange the exile.

96

But what to do with a people that still adored them? How to say to them good-bye we're leaving   enough of folkloric meals and little kisses you know where   enough my dears bye bye we are going   see you never send us postcards send representatives   write us notes good-bye we are tired of this humid air these interminable evenings looking down on you from the balcony of our presidential mansion the smell of these streets   the morning fog   the crunch of bread as we chew it all this wears us out and finishes us bye we want to shake the dust of this place off our shoes   the shops the styles the anniversaries and saints' days crimes of passion the taste of the first sweetheart we leave all that to you   lives on top of lives to sweat out in these streets without us because we're leaving we will go and leave you with a hole   a doubt   everything could have been otherwise with our spirit this country could have been saved

     THIS COUNTRY

     OUR COUNTRY

     THE FUTURE

we could have saved ourselves with more fiestas by opening more hospitals more hoaxes shown on television   my dears our lives have been a charade a farce   my dears there was nothing between us   we are going because this government has been a protracted dream and now we yearn for the true reality that comes at the end of a voyage   it has been a tremendous mistake   we will go by night   and we will write you and send you tapes.

THE CONSPIRATORS

Dear Carmela:

You don't know me but we have something important in common. I have a secret that I would like to share with you as soon as possible. I know that this will seem impertinent to you but don't be afraid, I am a respectable person and the benefits of our meeting will become evident as soon as we can talk together. Please come to the tea room La Ideal at quarter after five on Thursday afternoon. My name is Rosario and I will be wearing purple.

Till then, your

Rosario

Rosario Capodiluna

Carmela, carmelita, let's get out of the deadening aerobic rhythm, let's jump from one thing to the other, let's go to the appointment. Something is approaching. Something ends and suggests an avenue leading to the world of trysts and complications. Certainly I'll go, certainly after my shower and my little class I will put on my gray suit and go to meet the little girl in purple   this rosarito capodiluna who could she be, please? What does she want with me since for some time I have seen nobody?   Why since with my classes and my rock 'n roll my head has turned into a radio, who can she be the little girl in purple, would you also be interested in physical exercise? Would you also like to hang your cute little outfit in the locker?

A secret that turns out not to be one because Francisco is nothing to me now yes surely with his life as General and all that and Cristina but as for me the one I liked was fat Teitelbaum and what does it matter to me if

Francisco likes to dress up as a young girl; miss, please, miss let's use a little imagination   if he likes to be a girl you ought to enjoy being a general but I have forgotten all those things now   I have another life other pleasures. How ambitious Rosario   what a way to want to get ahead I suggest you relax and forget like me.

Let's dance dearest one the tea room has turned the lights out already and the dance floor has been lit up. With your purple dress. Let's dance aerobically. What do plans for the future matter? This moment is ours. How stiff your waist my dear you need some flexing exercises your body has become flabby from thinking about love so much   you need to dance   the great sweaty conga that will pass through you in an invigorating path. You look like a stocky statue   what loss of muscle tone, my dear, why?

Rosario danced until she got blisters on her feet; the red cross found her huddled in a corner of the tea room in the morning and when she returned home her mama greeted her by saying "see?"

END OF AN ERA

103

Black crepe, red flowers, downcast eyes. One by one the line advances. One has to offer homage, grant to the illustrious dead man the respect he deserves. Something of this atmosphere oozes out and pools between the toes. Steps grow leaden, our faces become grief-stricken, now we are the image of sadness that will appear in the morning papers. They will look at us and try to catch it. They will look at us and say   these are the men and women who make our country. If they have managed to call up these grave faces from their deepest fibers, produce them as example for us it means that something has happened in our lives beyond the ephemeral events of everyday, beyond the routine of the present. Can we come out of our lethargy and do the same? Forget about our bunions, the gas bill, this itching and come up with an expression of eternity so that the whole neighborhood can know, join in, and make the tragedy greater?

When Father Gabriel heard the news about Francisco's death it seemed too good to be true, like winning the daily double after the find of fat Teitelbaum's body. He added ice to the box, put in a bit more camphor water and danced around the room with his own shadow. He hugged and congratulated himself, sang joyful hymns to himself while he ironed his funeral cassock in order to go to the presidential mansion.

Remorseful, lying, the lucky priest goes to shake the hand of Madame Cristina, now he touches her, now winks at her but she takes no notice, so caught up she is in this event. She has imagined this moment of her life in so realistic a fashion that she can even distract herself from her future plans and concentrate on the stilled eyebrows of the General, devote her attention to the drawn look of his tightly closed lips.

Oh Cristina what are you going to do now with the trunks full of the General's clothes, what about your plans for england? how to get rid of his schoolgirl outfit? now they are all dead the witnesses and Francisco's little playmates all those who know of his tender hopes of little girl   only the ones who admired the sterile macho of the country remain, only them and Cristina who was racking her brains and arranging her hair in the style of a great lady because now she wanted to grow stronger in order to screw all her enemies with a minsk campaign that would bury them in oblivion and cure her immense loneliness.

Dear readers:

Of course long boring months of preparations and trivialities went by, of course it was necessary to move fat Teitelbaum from one place to another several times and the complicities that arose caused lifelong friends to betray one another, of course there was more corruption than ever and strikes threatened more than once to close the country down but of course Cristina's prestige kept growing as she stopped appearing in public, dedicated as she was to a total make-over for her imminent voyage to happiness.

Trunks   armoires   telephone calls   underclothes thrown out for being out of style   what kind do they wear over there?   who will see mine? leave the address book behind. Private airplanes zigzagging back and forth. Her exile after the military coup cleverly orchestrated by herself. Outside at last. In her element at last. Bye poor guttersnipes. Bye ass lickers. So long my comrades in arms.

EXILES

England opened like a misty flower. Men with raincoats and newspapers under their arms walked to work. Here indeed people smell good. Civilized country. Gray trousers. Straightforward glances. They go about their affairs as if they mattered because they do matter.

In this country it is easy to feel oneself a stranger. Let them think I am mysterious. Let them follow me and ask about where I come from. At last I can dress myself in proper style. I am from there. Now they will never impose a childhood on me or foretell my future. A total mystery for my neighbors. They will dream about me in the midst of their ingrained customs. They will want to break out of their routines but the price will be too high and most of them will remain forever fixed in their family portraits. Poor gnats trapped in their habits. Wrapped in their odors and maternities, these women will never know the pleasures of my helpless state, the fierce joy of my roaming.

OH, WHAT A HOWL

When she opened her trunks Cristina found only moth-eaten pieces of gray cloth. All of her preparations, being premature, had demolished her intended chicness and now here she was without money or relations in a shocking situation. But the general staff of the army had thought of everything when they condemned Cristina to madness. For years and years they had been building an underground universe in which her illusory exile could be played out; the muchachos had carried out innumerable and laborious kidnappings in order to pay for the long and endless galleries, shopping malls and simulated climates of various countries so that Cristina could move about the world forever like a toboggan, a banana peel. Francisco's death had plunged her into another eternity. They had to remove her from political ferocities, bury her alive without her realizing it and so make escape impossible.

Cristina in England. Cristina upset searching for some garment without holes when the friend appeared. I will help you, I will make you feel at home. I am part of the hotel staff. Friends, closest of friends. We'll start by singing some songs in English to practice. Let's sing and sew at the same time because we are hard-working people. We don't waste a minute.

—No, you pay nothing in this hotel. Everything free for Madame Cristina. We recognize the value of foreigners for our tourism industry. Have you ever heard of someone visiting a country where no one else goes? Most people would be afraid to be the only one; not everybody is as adventurous as Madame. How well they suit you the beggar-style clothes you are wearing. Here in England we have so little imagination, we are so methodical, isn't that right Madame?

At five in the afternoon, worn out from writing her memoirs, she would sit down in a tea shop to have a nice cup of tea with tiny little sandwiches cut in triangles. Night and day Cristina worked to get down on paper the scenes of this country so different from her own. She wants her writing to record like a camera but the act itself means nothing to her; she writes to forget where she came from; she writes to slough off the habits of her province.

Why, then, does she feel nervous when her voice reverberates in the sky as if it were closed in instead of out in the open? Why does she have the feeling that she has been set down in a service station? Who was there to miss? Who, if she had forgotten them already? Isn't there too much fog in England?

Through the window the voice of someone singing. Sounds of some child or other crying. So here in this house people connect with one another also. Our walls are porous the Friend said to her. Here in London we will live in anonymity. One can only be really famous in countries that have no national pride. We will stay here so that people will ignore us and only those closest to us will visit us. They will ask us for favors. They will distract us from the trappings in which distance has submerged us.

Seated on crimson hassocks Cristina and the Friend awaited the visitors, who surprised them with questions about their personal lives eyes glinting with curiosity and as they responded they looked down modestly inspecting their fingernails. It was an impressive scene: their riding clothes of English tweeds; the canapés of white cheese and pepper, the portrait of the queen of England smiling at them from the wall; the muchachos were bowled over by the immediate success of their conspiracies. Cristina loved the Friend; she forgot about her own murderous talents and, in her cherished captivity, seemed not to suspect the limitations of her fantastic exile.

But it goes without saying that the muchachos were greedy and in the hustle and bustle world of those enamored of distance, such a perfect exile ought to yield agreeable sums, enough to cause the pockets of their tight pants to bulge with pride and to inject the necessary desire into much-loved vaginas. So it was, for the love of sheets, while clasping in their arms young girls dazzled by the dream of a gilded future, that the muchachos selected a delegation that would travel throughout the world to collect companions for Cristina.

Very soon the cost of exile became part of the military budget of any

110

nation that could boast of a healthy number of intrigues. STRONG COUNTRY OFFERING GOOD EXILE OPTIONS read the top secret propaganda fliers that the muchachos circulated around the bases of most interest to them. Without any doubt, the campaign of submission of the dictators was one of the most important feats in the political career of Rodrigo de León, a real macho type with black eyes and beard smelling depressingly of rotten fish. From the garage where he repaired trucks after leaving his fish store, Rodrigo de León supervised the shipping of materials needed to make the exile a perfect dream. Make sure there are enough draftees dressed in business suits to fill the streets; don't forget to add one or two dog turds at the corner so that Cristina could look at her friend and exclaim: "see? even here they have garbage" and above all, make sure that the specially printed newspapers had photographs of Cristina, each one more respectful than the last, holding fast to her Friend's hand and that the captions speak of her place of origin as a distant location already disappeared.

Although Rodrigo de León was a son of a bitch, in that period he also had some good qualities that might not hit you in the eye but were nevertheless obvious to those who had close contact with him. At about thirty years of age he had learned to talk and when he became the spiritual architect of exile, his vocabulary already amounted to more than a hundred words. The enthusiasm with which he stockpiled materials in the galleries went hand in hand with the growth of his linguistic supply; Cristina lived in the animated dictionary of Rodrigo de León. When he got interested in geography things became somewhat more problematical. They would have to convince Cristina to change countries, get the Friend to tell her tales to persuade her that a more interesting world existed in another direction, they would have to build more galleries, astound her once again. But Cristina was so enchanted with her new austerity, so pleased with the bitter taste of orange marmalade that everything seemed perfect to her and the delegations of muchachos who came to praise the world of the Caribbean were disdainfully received and dismissed by a Cristina more and more her own person, so much so that she had forgotten the language they once had in common.

SOMEWHERE,
OVER THE RAINBOW . . .

When the games of exile became tiresome for the local muchachos, the chorus of illiterate women from the school of the holy conception showed up to enliven the evenings of the lady. They were poor women picked up from the streets where they had been abandoned like kittens in doorways of asylums when they were barely born and whose ignorance was maintained by means of strict spiritual exercises intended to keep hidden the impurity that had brought them into the world. Concealed in the black skirts of one of them, a very young boy arrived who had heard exaggerated stories about the riches of exile. He came determined to conquer and to acquire power, head dizzy from so many religious chants and ears disgusted by the odd accent of the illiterate women who had never spoken to anyone except the nuns of their school and one another.

For Cristina it was enough to glimpse the procession of gray women in their dark clothes to know that one phase of her life had ended. Silhouetted against the background of neon lights imitation Covent Garden, the two hundred murmuring figures knitting rapidly as they walked, beckoned Cristina to leave the Friend, to hang up the tailored suit and surrender to the humiliation of begging. When Tomás, the boy, let out a fart, the group stopped cold. The knitting suddenly ceased, the needles pointing toward the ground, a shout of horror emerged from the crowd. Among these women nobody had ever farted. None of them had ever eaten anything fatty, voluptuous and heavy enough to give rise to the loving and vexing gas that interferes with motion and relieves the body. It was as though a wall had suddenly become a window, or as if a chimney had started to puff out perfectly formed smoke rings. Cristina stopped in the middle of taking off her suit and said, with firm voice: "that child needs a laxative."

"maría cristina wants to boss me around
and I follow her, I follow her lead
so later people won't say that
maría cristina bosses me around"

The illiterate women chanted day and night in their dialect that sounded like crickets. They went walking through the London exile, in four regular columns of fifty with their woolen handwork, knitting knitting like mad the same clothes they were wearing, so that their uniform was never changed. Their voices astounded Cristina who wanted to wheedle from the Friend the sense of this procession, to join it herself to find out what they were chanting, to understand their message. However, it was impossible because the sense of the speech of the two hundred virgins together was not intelligible to any doll dressed in the height of fashion.

Tomás, purged and on a diet, acquired such agility that he was able to climb to the peak of the only London mountain and finally, after much effort, he managed to touch a violet colored cloud made of such inferior cardboard that it yielded immediately to the pressure of his fingers making a little hole through which a constant stream of damp earth began to fall. He had discovered that exile was a cardbord illusion and now, full of enthusiasm over the idea of building an enormous sand castle with stellar dirt, promised himself to return right after supper with a pail and shovel.

CATACOMBS

It had never occurred to Rodrigo de León to bury the dictators alive. What interested him was the business part, getting out of the fish store appealed to him, and to be able to send young Tomás to college after a brief apprenticeship in exile; he did not want the glory that the armies of the world were conferring on him at this moment nor did he have the usual material aspirations fueled by the money that flowed into his coffers, funds extorted by ardent revolutionaries who wanted to fill more boats with more and more rulers longing for safe exile, double locked, provided at the same time that not a single drop of BLOOD BE SHED. He didn't want all this and yet, his recent friendship with Father Gabriel had made him recognize how important it was for the country, it could be turned into the touristic marvel of the universe, the ideal place for newlyweds to spend their honeymoon, for first communion celebrations, and why not? for solemn and respectful funerals of heads of state who owed their happiness and short reigns to the inventive talents of Rodrigo de León.

So when the troupe of Scottish acrobats came back terrified, because they had seen the beginning of the crumbling set off by Tomasito's little finger, Rodrigo de León developed a stomach ulcer that stayed with him for the rest of his life. Soldiers from foreign nations were brought in, subjected to campaigns of disinformation so that they wouldn't know what they were excavating, and work began to free the disconcerted world about to disappear beneath the earth.

—Don't be angry, my fat friend, little ruskie with your frozen navel, don't be so stiff I've already given you more ice, my blue and purple prince charming. Still, stonestill and swollen minskian Teitelbaum. Soon our time will come. Be patient while I spruce you up and hide you. That's how Father Gabriel talked to fat Teitelbaum who was now kept in a box below the Father's own bed. Father Gabriel had formed the habit of sleeping in several layers of underclothes since the frozen vapor rising from the floor went right through his bones. The cleaning woman thought his aches were due to his age and begged him please to allow her to clean his miserable little room, argued that the vow of poverty had been fulfilled by now and that the ones of work and humility were not so important because after all nobody would have the nerve to call him lazy after all these years with all he was doing to help in the process of national reconstruction, so hand in glove as he was now with the new group of muchachos in power, so cheek by jowl with this one and that one, those who mattered. "No, no and no; thank you very much, I will do it myself."

When the dirt first began to fall over the little sandwiches of white cheese it looked like a bit of caviar overflowing from heaven, another british refinement, reinforcing the sense of wellbeing that distance brings, but when the painful truth of the crumbling was made evident by thick fistfuls, then clumps of garbage that had been accumulating for years and perhaps centuries, there was no room for doubt; the sky was falling on their heads; the apocalypse had reached europe and it was time to run, take cover, make tracks.

—We were closer to everything and therefore also closer to the end of the world.

—In my country time does not pass, they only speak of going backward, of crisis. We believe we are eternal. These are the convulsions of progress.

—Inexorably toward the end. Because everything that is ordained must end to make way for the dust that we will always be. This is our eternity.

While the ex-dictators sitting in their bright colored leather chairs were speculating on the events breaking out in the northern galleries, having no hope of saving themselves yet in their optimistic moments praising this common burial that brought them together where the power of so many nations would remain posthumously united, Cristina and the Friend were running through galleries still intact where the cardboard still looked like solid sky.

They ran and ran behind the two hundred virgins, their knitting forgotten and their skirts hiked up, fleeing from the open air where they sensed death; they ran without singing and barely breathing, recognizing themselves by their sweat and almost confessing that the artificial breezes and storms that they now yearned for, wrought by the imagination of Rodrigo de León, was their lost paradise. Out of breath the contingent arrived at a barrier, an enormous wall with a heavy door. Young Tomás, at the head of the group, turned the doorknob and a spectacular landscape opened before their eyes resplendent with guacamayos, green trees, sand, beach and summer vacationers in bikinis surfing.

They had arrived at the second stage of the voyage by accident. There was not yet anyone to receive them; the employees—all Arabs—had never heard of the Friend or Cristina. Rodrigo de León had had this pavilion built for the kidnapped where it was always warm and always day; there was no way to measure time. It was a luminous catacomb without mirrors where the young draftees served a hitch of only three weeks so they would not become accustomed to the pleasures of the enormous tropical murals, the warm air conditioning, the white teeth of drunken tourists practicing water sports.

The virgins, in perfect formation in front of the beach immediately took up their knitting and went back to their murmuring litany but Cristina and the Friend, emboldened by their flight and fed up with so many serious voices, quickly threw off their london clothes and, stark naked, began to shout: LEPER WOMEN LEPER WOMEN GET OUT OF HERE.

In the general affability of the catacomblike retreat, the establishment of a leprosarium was like a gigantic wart, a stain that could not be erased, a place that no draftee or hostage would dare to explore.

The two hundred virgins, ignorant of the reasons for their isolation, went on living the way they always had, together, eating worms and tatters of wool, tirelessly dedicated to their work. From the perspective of their eyes, used to looking downward so as not to drop a single stitch and to find insects to eat, this phase was, in truth, a privilege. They enjoyed the centipedes, the plump bugs natural to the little piece of land where they lived, surrounded by an enormous mosquito net supported by palm trees. The gentleness of this internment did not escape them and in the evening, at the hour when even in this unmoving world, the body longed for rest, they regressed, let out a collective sigh, two hundred babies peaceful at last.

The tourists had no choice but to pass by the leprosarium on their way to the piano bar for their daily piña coladas, margaritas and flirtations but they did it with a certain feeling of unease that they did not dare admit to their companions; they quickened their steps, adjusted their sunglasses and whistled songs that had been popular in their countries of origin before they were kidnapped and plunged into their Caribbean eternity. In the bars they never spoke of the events that had brought them together. They pretended to have no interest in what was happening outside, nor to remember the humiliation of having been snatched from their daily oc-cupations by strangers who, after months of torture and interrogations, had sent them to this subterranean and luminous hideaway. They carried out their roles as tourists perfectly and had even developed a solid ethic of resistance. They discussed among each other the cowardice typical of the hostages who gave in to torture, the lack of civic responsibility of those who did not manage to deceive their handlers or learn their language well enough so that at the necessary moment they could mingle with them.

They talked and talked. They congratulated each other and invented extraordinary circumstances to demonstrate the courage they had showed in face of danger. They organized COURSES OF DIGNITY and awarded as prizes minute pebbles they picked up dutifully from the beach amid laughs, jabs in the ribs and half-understood jokes. Obviously the lie of their explicit convictions would have to come out at night while they slept and dreamed of their true identities as the vanquished. But in the cheerful hideaway of a garishly painted Caribbean without the darkness that invites uncertainty, the hostages posing as tourists were incapable of introspection. One draftee who managed to smuggle in a camera took pictures of the ball games on the beach and of people he met in the piano bar. When he showed them proudly to his fiancée she made him promise to take her there on their honeymoon.

Cristina and the Friend were naked and had no way of buying themselves bikinis because Rodrigo de León, who was at bottom very puritanical, had strictly forbidden any trade in the Caribbean zone of exile, fearing that the mingling of hostages and ex-dictators might bring about an amoral and dissolute society. Cristina suddenly became conscious of how thin she was; the Friend stayed hunched over at first but later realized that even without clothes Cristina would not spot her as a spy and would keep on confiding to her one after the other all the secrets of her wide sway of power with Francisco.

What better way to hide than to come out into the open, exposing oneself to the tourists' glances until they were accepted as part of the landscape that went with paid vacations? Hieratic and erect, noble, one looking toward the east, hand raised elegantly over the head of the other who was crouching as if searching for a lost button, they turned into living statues

on the beach. That way it was logical that they not wear clothes. Even the
Arab captors passed them by without looking at them, paying no attention
to their nude bodies. Garbed by the imagination of their own art, Cristina
and the Friend spent various days spinning plans for their future. They did
not feel as carefree as the rest of the Caribbean population. After all they
had seen the beginning of the European apocalypse and felt they ought to
tell about it, let the others know that the packaged happiness they were
enjoying could crumble at any moment. Since their bodies were lily white
due to the protection of tweed, they seemed like marble statues and even
they themselves shivered from the cold, affected by their own pose, true
artists, magnificent, almost without breathing.

THE FREE LIFE

—"One, two, three, four . . ."

—"Twenty-eight, twenty-nine thousand, forty million . . ."

The economy was in crisis. Bus tickets had gone up so much that each passenger, armed with a suitcase full of money, had to spend long periods of time counting out the ever fluctuating amounts to pay the fare for a ride that was invariably late and unpredictable.

Beauty contests proliferated in a country that no longer believed in material advantages. The nationalized chain of cosmetic products, HERE TODAY GONE TOMORROW, the only consistently successful business in the carnage of the time, sponsored contests among all sectors of the population. The prizes were not as attractive as the general admiration enjoyed by the winners and the prestige gained from the showy tattoos that were applied to the forehead in a public ceremony instead of a crowning.

But let's not fool ourselves, dear friends, children and teen-agers: all this was a sideshow that the muchachos in power had invented to help the time pass while they continued their nightly hunts that filled the city with tortured bodies, corpses floating in the river, moans of lovers snatched from their caresses to undergo fierce political and personal interrogations that led nowhere. Because the muchachos had forgotten why they wanted to make the prisoners talk, what they wanted to prove, how they should record their activities. Bloodthirsty, they kept insisting on details that they noted down in huge ledgers so as not to appear negligent.

What color suit was uncle Antonio wearing the day of your confirmation; why didn't your aunt Elena come to the party and who was the guy who gave you the receipt and bill for the sandwiches for the reception in the courtyard? How is it possible that you don't remember? communist son of a bitch, how is it possible since it's written down in the earlier ledger? tell me what you are hiding from us   tell us everything   every little thing with all the details   what was the telephone number of your music teacher   and what time of day would she come? what do I care if it happened a long time ago   if it happened you ought to remember it right?   don't keep any secrets here because we've got plenty to do.

Here we have plenty to do   we are busy people   tell us you conniving sons of bitches   tell us how many times you went to that doctor and what he wrote on the prescriptions   the name of the pharmacy and why the man who worked there got divorced the week he sold you the medicine everything is connected   everything is related   let's make a note let's make a note   no no don't clean up the blood   damn it   that way they know   that way they realize that nobody plays games with the authorities   nobody hides anything   let's keep very careful records put that one in a bag and throw him in the river   he could hardly stand anything   he was barely able to remember the name of his first grade teacher   people with no guts   no brains   nothing   unpatriotic   un-caring

Each one trying to outdo the other   each one more brutal   more ingenious in thinking up ways to violate bodies   to provoke screams. The muchachos did their job very well, they were afraid that someone would realize that no one knew any longer what they were supposed to find out and why; they knew that if the cat got out of the bag there would go all the extras: WATCHES   STEREOS   STYLISH CLOTHES   MONEY   to say noth-ing of the excitement of going out on the nightly chase   let's see who'll we grab today   that one   that peabrain   he thinks he's just strolling down the street arm around his little sweetheart   and that one there that woman is surely up to no good   let's check out this apartment house   something good should be cooking here   there'll be enough to go around   the city belongs to us   better than drinking a case of wine better than fucking a whole regiment   let's go hunting   we'll give them a thrashing they'll never forget and build a country. The muchachos were afraid. They were hungry. They wanted to show their mettle, become men, gain the respect of others. Little by little each one broke with girlfriend, family, playing pool and became totally absorbed by the nightly obsession, the perfecting of their techniques, the game of questions and answers. Swallowed up by a logic that they no longer understood, victims of the emptiness of their lives, in the cold and rainy nights of winter someone suggested that there was a traitor among them and then all of them turned on the guy chanting   SQUEAL STOOLIE SQUEAL   PUT HIM ON THE GRILL WHERE EVERYBODY SQUEALS and laughing and spitting they tied him down, goosed him here and there with the electric prods then turned him loose after several hours to sit down all together to eat the juicy steak with french fries that always awaited them when the sessions were over.

Nobody in the country wanted to talk about the muchachos. Everybody was inclined to wonder about them and some even suspected that a certain very nice neighbor became one of them by night. "He is just moonlighting to support his family," the concierge whispered; "he does it because he is a degenerate, they are all like that," "he doesn't do it, he must have inherited some money," "I think that car he uses is to distribute contraband". . . The shame of silence kept growing among the people; they felt it when they went to the movies, at birthday parties, every time they had to cross the street to avoid hearing the shrieks coming from some place of interrogation carelessly set up in an emergency detention center, every time that, even in a hurry, they would get off the bus when they believed they spotted one of the muchachos inside.

They lived like tiles of a Byzantine mosaic, each one trying to keep to its own color and occupation without knowing the pattern of the whole, kept going by an iron faith in god   unseeing unhearing. Shards of mosaic with the willpower of gnats. Everybody wanted to leave. Everybody dreamed of taking off but never said so because in public the muchachos were superpatriots; they were strong and their swashbuckling manner wiped out anything that seemed foreign.

The children grew up playing ball, hide-and-seek, telling riddles giving no sign of what was coming, not letting on to the distracted group in power that they were making meticulous plans for an invasion from the parks, kindergartens and even high schools. Some mothers noticed it because of the disdainful way the babies looked at their breasts and the smiles they exchanged only with each other. Aside from that everything was normal, they let themselves be decked out in little sailor suits and laces, they celebrated patriotic holidays and even wrote compositions that made the eyes of the school authorities fill with tears. No doubt about it, this was a country on the move whose citizens once again knew what discipline was, had a sense of duty and a healthy fear of the consequences of their actions.

At that time Rosario, who was taking care of Tomasito in Rodrigo de León's house because of the premature death of his mother, was kept handcuffed to a post in the patio, her hair lank and dirty from rain and sun, her lithe body weakened and her mouth dry from repeating over and over to Rodrigo de León that she didn't know where his son was, that he simply did not come back one day from an errand. She soon reached the conclusion that life was indeed a vale of tears and that being so it was better not to add any more complaints to the ones already existing; one morning she woke up and began to sing romantic songs that she composed in her sleep. Rodrigo de León started compelling her to sing every morning and every night, he fed her with birdseed to protect her throat, put up a canopy for her so that she would no longer get wet and bought her an enormous cage big enough so she could walk around and stretch her limbs when she wanted to do some exercises.

Bittybird, pretty bird, sing me a nice song ninnybird, skinny ninnybird, where is Tomás my only son? bittybird my picture pretty bird   a bolero one that tells of ivy and crosses by the roadside, bittybird, ninnybird of my dreams.

Rosario developed a sharp intuition about what Rodrigo wanted. Soon she found him so melancholy, so dependent on her tunes that it was enough to make one trill for him to present her with succulent dishes especially prepared to nourish her voice; he gave her rings and bracelets that the soldiers brought him in payment for expenses incurred by their exile program for dictators. He turned miserly, no longer listened to the customers who came into the fish store; he was bored by their recipes for cod à la portuguaise, their red nails bothered him and the pride they showed when speaking of their children.

Bittybird, ninnybird, how I long to cradle you in my arms; ninnybird pretty little songbird let's go to sleep bunting bird   sweetsweet love song ladybird how I long to show you   adorn you   caress you

Rosario would run from one corner of her cage to the other, make ready to take wing and sing some bolero that told of inevitable loss ending in the death of one of the two lovers by the side of the road; Rodrigo would leave, ashamed, with his hands folded over his fly cursing the moment he had offended his bittybird, promising himself never again to fall into such common behavior, never again to give in to the dirty passions of his body.

Rosario didn't know that by cleansing him of all sexual desire, she was avenging herself for the humiliation she suffered at the hands of Francisco. At last she was happy; her cage became her shield, she trilled and trilled her triumphant tunes, her spectacular victory in a battle that, as she now knew, would be waged without quarter.

Chatterchatter my teeth chattering out of my head. Legs trembling, arthritis in every joint. Hastening on, ruination my age. Now there's nobody to remember me when I was a schoolboy with knees made for soccer, running, the cold of short pants.

Chatterchatter with this shitty ice that I have to put on you to keep you from smelling, so that nobody will suspect, so that they won't disturb our little plan. Even so, you with your spectacular belly and gold teeth and eyebrows of rich old man, the fat from so much gorging in the best restaurants, even so I have the advantage over you because I am alive, bright-eyed and bushy-tailed thanks to this country in mourning. Minsk, my bedroom, Minsk beneath my bed, Minsk is the kingdom of my will. I will arrange your resurrection whenever I wish, they will dance a conga around us; they will treat us like VIPs, we will settle the fiercest strikes, we will return the country to calm with the surprise of our arrival.

They will look at us astounded.

We will pose for the photographers.

They will give you a new suit.

Hundreds and hundreds of women will come to make confessions with new sins, interesting ones, they will dream of your frozen prick, they will feel like sibyls, they will ask me for exorcisms, they will pray, desperate souls night and day; there will be no empire greater than my confessional booth.

Dear readers, male and female, uncles and cousins:

Greed had sunk its claws into Father Gabriel; he was dazzled by the possibility of rising to the very height of power. He did not realize how vulgar his fantasies were, and in the meantime, he managed to catch a terrible cold that not even his wool socks could prevent. He didn't know, as we do, that the most important thing in this life is to be nice and warm in a cozy bed, with familiar smells, a friendly pillow and feet snug beneath the blanket.

She came jumping a rope wearing striped cotton socks and little white batiste panties that you could see every time she turned the rope.

—Good morning, good morning, excuse me for being forward but I am Tomasito's girlfriend. It's been quite a while since he came to the park and I miss him, he was my protector, my pal, nobody like him for jumping and racing and seeing how many ice cream cones one could eat in three minutes. I'd like to know if he is sick, if he needs anything, if he has moved, if he has found his lost mother finally, I would like to know how he is and that's why I didn't go to school today and came here to the fish store instead because a boyfriend is a serious matter. Tomasito and I have known each other forever. I am waiting for him, I miss him, I get confused and think it's him when I see a skinny kid come walking along in the distance. Please, tell me, pay attention to me, and if you don't remember now, here is my address: Celeste Rodríguez, right across from the bakery, come anytime, don't call on the telephone because nobody in my house knows anything. See you soon and excuse me for bothering you, very nice of you, don't shut the door in my face, you've been so good to your son all these years mother and father but now he has a girlfriend and the minute he appears I will take care of him, I'll take him away from here and we'll play house, age doesn't matter, only the love that binds us, imagine ever since kindergarten our schoolteachers have been saying that we would get married someday; he must have told you something, although with your constant worry about the fish store who knows if you had time to listen to him; I have always spoken well of you, even now with rumors going around about caged women in your house, talk about witchcraft and nonsense, but always, always, always I spoke well of you because I feel like part of the family already.

Rodrigo de León went back to being the same as ever after Celeste's visit. In ten minutes he had raped Rosario with such indifference and abandon that he forgot to close the door of the cage as he left, with resigned step, to make the telephone call that would end Celeste's life and her threat to turn Tomasito into a contented and mediocre little boyfriend. Rosario flapped her arms, slipped through the open door of the cage, and with new-found agility in her legs, climbed to the top of the highest tree on the street. Erect as an eagle, but fragile as a sparrow, she couldn't yet gauge distances when an irresistible desire overcame her, ordering her to jump, to fly or to fall, to play the final card.

Nobody saw her fall into the garbage truck, mingle with the city's trash, nobody heard the limpid trill of her farewell nor noticed the slight disarray caused by her body. Her mama had already buried her some time ago, since the episode with Francisco. "My daughter is a strange bird" she had said to herself; her father missed her throughout many twilight evenings because he had perceived in her a capacity for fiasco unequaled only by his own. The organizers of the beauty contest HERE TODAY GONE TOMOR-ROW tried unsuccessfully to find her to give her a prize, consecrate her as their icon of the day, show off her perfect skin before the cameras.

Now nobody could prevent the strikes that were paralyzing the country. No work in the factories. No pasta, meat or marmalade in the stores. The whole country ate only snacks available in the countless kiosks that stayed open, unaffected by the work stoppages. A black market of chocolates and other candies introduced a different currency: everything was paid for in bonbons, chewing gum, popcorn. The people became hyperactive because of their sugary diet. Now they no longer slept or followed any normal schedule. JOIN THE STRIKE   DOWN WITH EXPLOITERS   LET'S SING   LET'S DEMONSTRATE   LET'S DECLARE WAR ON OUR ENEMIES   chanted men, women and children marching in mass demonstrations that always ended on some corner where they could stock up on more snacks and then everything dissolved into revels, carnivals and music festivals.

Father Gabriel felt the patriotic itch. His moment had come at last. It was necessary to find a way out of the situation, to return to order, start up once again the endless chain of obligations and sadnesses that would guarantee the future of paradise, inferno and the family. But he was failing; his arthritis, aggravated by chocolate, meant he could not carry out his mission alone. That's how he happened to send a woman with a message to Rodrigo de León's house. She found him transformed; no more fish smell in his beard so he had quit wrinkling up his nose, and his new diet, because of the loss of quite a few teeth, made him look like a benevolent patriarch. With more flesh than muscle, a less stubborn will and a freer laugh, Rodrigo de León followed her to Father Gabriel's little room. He had to dodge through the crowds dancing in the church where marriages were celebrated one after the other amid guffaws and farts. As he entered the room where Father Gabriel was waiting, he couldn't help shivering. It was as though winter had come all of a sudden. Once his eyes grew accustomed to the darkness, he could make out the figure of Father Gabriel squatting beside the body of fat Teitelbaum.

Warmth.   Complicity.   Opportunities. Vast, enormous possibilities, the excitement of his new friendship electrified Rodrigo de León. Suddenly he felt like a new person, forgotten now Celeste, Rosario, Tomasito and his long string of misfortunes since the day when a boatload of African dictators sank minutes before docking in exile leaving behind an inexplicable mass of fat bejewelled bodies as a feast for the sharks, tame up to then, but who afterwards began to attack every boat brave enough to set sail. With a light heart Rodrigo began to sing:

> homeland   sweet homeland   your pop's a happy man
> here I bring you something grand
> homeland   sweet homeland   I lead you by the hand

Cheap, cheap his song is cheap, slummy soul, spawned in a shantytown, stupid if you think I am going to turn over my precious corpse with no strings attached. Stop singing and dancing bushy beard, fake revolutionary, I don't want money, I want recognition, crowds, to dress in fancy clothes, to be the confidant of technical virgins, pickpockets who snatch wallets on buses, children masturbated by maiden aunts. Stop singing, idiot, you'll wake up the rats, and let's make plans for this hotshot festival. I'm not interested in your skill in preserving fish by freezing. Fatty here has already turned into a statue. He has ice inside, I have been feeding him crushed ice for months, I have embalmed him inside and outside and I have even brushed his teeth every day. Cleaner than when his mama spiffed him up in Minsk. More pompous than when he dressed up for one of his gala parties.

They talked in low voices; patted each other on the back and planned everything with a great luxury of details. They took him out by themselves after issuing a call on radio and TV for people to come to the plaza for a mass meeting. They would put him on a throne, announce his will that everybody go back to work, that the country return to humility, fatigue, to the rhythm of factories that opened at seven in the morning. Once again the cities would smell of soup prepared with fish and vegetables instead of the greasy fumes of the snacks, once again the muchachos would be put in charge of maintaining order, although they were somewhat rowdy, they had managed with their crude methods to scare the population who should start once again to produce things for export, for the maintenance of roads, for newspapers, now without anything at all to report. THIS IS THE ANTHEM OF THE RETURN. LET US COME BACK TO OUR COUNTRY.   WE HAVE BEEN AWAY FOR MANY LONG MONTHS MAYBE YEARS   WE HAVE MISSED THE LOVING YOKE OF OUR LEADERS FRANCISCO AND THE GREAT LADY BUT LET US COME BACK   COME BACK   WITH THE BEST OF THEM   WITH THEIR FAVORITE EXQUISITE MASTER OF CEREMONIES FAT TEITELBAUM LET US LISTEN TO HIS WISHES AS WE USED TO EVERY DAY   WITH TELE-VISION SETS TURNED ON LET US LISTEN TO HIS WILL   LET HIM TELL US WHAT HE YEARNS FOR   I WILL SPEAK FOR HIM   HE WILL GUIDE US BACK TO OUR NATION

Because a country needs a guide to be a nation   a country should abolish dances   in order to get ahead a country needs a person in uniform to point the way   a country is something special   something great   in-finite   that we ought to build in our imagination every morning when we get up   a country ought to celebrate patriotic holidays   inculcate in children respect for boredom   a smooth-running country cares for its dead   venerates   its   forefathers   cares   cares about dignity   fos-ters cold judgment   common sense   marriages performed in the church now that is a country   a country needs a leader who does not lose his

head   who does not change   who is coherent   our leader   our model
is fat Teitelbaum and we speak for him.

How they practiced for their performance. How carefully they chose their
clothes. What an impressive pair. Father Gabriel with a glistening cassock
newly starched and ironed and Rodrigo de León, wearing his most resplendent fishmonger's apron. They learned their speeches by heart. They
cleaned their nails and gargled with the white of an egg so that their
throats would obey the impetus of their words.

On the appointed day they went out onto the balcony of the presidential
residence to make the announcement and to show fat Teitelbaum to the
crowd. Nobody heard the words so well rehearsed. The people had come
to the meeting because the fliers spread around the city at dawn had
promised a big prize for those who came and the crowd was clamoring for
more treats, they wanted to know if it was true that imported chocolates
were going to be distributed, and ices made of natural fruits that had been
missing for a long time now since nobody was willing to harvest the fruit
necessary to make them. They clamored and clamored for their sweets
with the insistence that only insomnia can give. This was a country that
never closed its eyes night or day, without the balance that comes from the
rhythms of waking and sleeping or the wisdom conferred by a diet of
vegetables. Father Gabriel was the first to realize that things were not
going according to plan, and in the middle of his speech of return, he
dropped the arm of fat Teitelbaum and fled into the street to mingle with
the crowd. Rodrigo de León, slower on the uptake, couldn't keep fat
Teitelbaum from falling forward and hanging suspended from the balcony.
Five minutes went by before Rodrigo realized that if he didn't run they
were likely to lynch him and he also took to his heels to arrange his affairs
and go into exile.

These measures were, naturally, quite unnecessary. The people were no longer vengeful. The chubby men and women with their teeth rotting out went on cheerfully exchanging packages of candy in front of the enormous body of fat Teitelbaum dangling from the balcony wanting to fall to mingle with the gentle people below who hardly paid him any attention at all.

WATERWORKS

First it came from the mouth. A reddish fluid as if the entrails had liquified. The rain fell over the crowd erasing the smiles from their faces. Then water began to flow from every orifice, in colors of bodily depths never before seen in public. Ochres, purplish browns, cloudy yellows. Death so long lived by fat Teitelbaum at last realized in threads of water and violent gushes. All liquid. Not a single bone left in his body. Not a single drop of fat that didn't fall to the pavement of the streets.

He neither fell nor moved. He simply dissolved into a puddle; his suit and the rest of his clothes carried toward the gutters by the personal cataract into which Father Gabriel had turned him.

Now sure they cry. Now sure they realize. Now sure they want to know what happened. They stop eating their sweets. Tiredness settles into their bones for good. They would have liked to see. To know. It happened in front of their eyes but they were unable to perceive it. Shame. Shame. Shame.

There is no deeper mourning than this. All the dead converge on them. Names forgotten; routines lost that used to connect them; lacking calendars, their history just went down the drain.

  —Did you see anything?
  —I was distracted.

There are no witnesses for an event that everybody saw. The miracle of their refound sadness escapes them for good. These people have grown old, they have reached the faded flower of their age.

WHERE DO THEY GO
THE ONES WHO WENT

"though you may wander long / you'll always hear my song / the strong cords of our love / will outlast every wrong . . ."

Music was played in the Caribbean exile constantly throughout the perpetual day. In the distance they could hear thunder, crumblings, the noise of England being carried away by the avalanche set off by Tomasito. But here so far there was still food wrapped in cellophane and served on little trays stolen from hijacked airplanes. The peacekeeping force had cut telephone communication with the handlers due to the avalanche but nobody was aware of it. The regular routine, the interrogations in the bar disguised as conversations, everything kept going on as usual.

The hostages were happy in their fashion. The trivialization of their lives had yielded immediate results. Once the hope of being liberated was lost they took on the virtues of lazy slaves. Inventing jokes, making fun of the draftees behind their backs, imitating the routines of the oriental dancers with their complicated belly gyrations. And they all learned the vulgar guffaw almost spit out that they could offer like a password to their captors.

At bottom, obviously, the draftees only wanted to go back home to normalize the situation with their sweethearts, who knows, entangled by now with other guys perhaps a little older and with hair on their chests. Once in a while a draftee would disappear and not come back, and although hopeful rumors of successful AWOLs made the rounds, everybody knew that the one who disappeared had succumbed to curiosity about the leprosarium and that now he was stuck in the jumbled world stirring beneath the white mosquito net.

—I don't want to stay in this position any longer because my bones are killing me, Cristina said to the Friend.

—Shh . . . Tell me a little more of what you remember of your life with Francisco, who advised you, who were the fashion designers you liked best, tell me again about that business of the first wife, what do you know about her and is she perhaps mixed up in politics? Do you think she had some connection with the military?

> Who were they
> Where did they live
> When and on what day and with whom
> A complete list
> Everything that you can recall

—But none of that matters to me any more and I don't remember anything about it; I can't stand this exile as statue any longer. Why do you ask me so many questions? Let's not talk. Let's jump off this pedestal, nobody will notice, let's go to another country, let's steal some clothes. Even if it's only a bikini. Let's go to some other European country. I find it delightful that countries are like shopping malls. You have no idea how boring it was the wind forever playing havoc with my hairdo; the changing seasons that meant you had to buy new outfits; let's look for some sort of transportation. Let's strike up a friendship with somebody.

But the Friend was too caught up in perfecting her interrogation technique. When she went back she would be greeted like a queen; all the political parties would seek her out as a consultant. Friend and confidante, depository of lists of names and places. She had to work fast, take advantage of the godsend of their immobility and amass data, service stripes, ribbons and medals that would become symbols of her power. Then no more interrogations. No more lists paid for by the yard. No more blood splatters to remember. Finally, life would turn into her version of happiness: a merry-go-round.

Rodrigo de León managed to catch up with Father Gabriel very quickly and to convince him that exile didn't require so much luggage. Dressed as British schoolmistresses they started on the trek that led below, toward the cave of concealment. Father Gabriel felt that at last he was about to attain glory, an existence in catacombs devoted to God after freeing himself from the jew Teitelbaum. His heart swelled with memories of pages that had led him to take religious vows, he carried with him a little whip for self-flagellation and a cassock cleverly hidden among the pleats of his tweed skirt.

Now he melted with tenderness for fat Teitelbaum, called him his saviour, the evil that had helped him to rise from this world to another, his one-way ticket to paradise. He congratulated himself for being able to withstand the cold, for the illusion of power, that, unbeknownst to him, had brought him to this instant, for Rodrigo de León, his guide, and for his closeness to water, fish, with the science of symbols . . .

—Shut your mouth, you shitty old man or I'll shut it for you, Rodrigo de León said to him, uncomfortable in his cashmere sweater and disoriented without his beard. Shut up and walk faster, or I'll walk right over you and bust your ass, keep walking and stop yakking, disgusting cohort; I am a victim of circumstances; I, a real macho, patriarch of the muchachos, stuck with a little greenhorn parish priest; get going, we have to find the path before it gets completely dark.

The avalanche had so completely demolished Rodrigo de León's elaborate English scenery that their descent was instantaneous. They fell through an immense hole to the very center of the old empire. Very little was left of it now. Rubbing his eyes, Rodrigo de León saw remains of ads for sales at Harrods, recognized the smell of dozens of spoiled kidney pies being devoured now by rats with glittering eyes; saw the dismembered bodies of draftees still holding paper cones of fish 'n chips in their hands; posters of business establishments in Oxford Street mingled with stones that belonged to some other vocabulary that he had forgotten by now. Confused, dirty, openly aggrieved by their fate, Rodrigo de León and Father Gabriel realized that the time had come to ditch their disguises as British schoolmistresses. Half naked they rolled downdowndown, part of the avalanche that now let go with a vengeance. Huddled in the fetal position they tumbled down but yelled like men, calling for help, hoping that one of the draftees or exiles would recognize their voices and offer them asylum in the Caribbean, or better yet, help them climb back up to freedom.

—This is my personal purgatory, it is my fate now I am dying for sure, now for sure I saw it coming . . . Father Gabriel ended up feeling sorry for Rodrigo de León who, during a respite in their fall, wrapped him up being careful to leave him a breathing space, and carried him along like a little bundle to be his companion and adversary.

Let us picture their travails, their fears, their ravaged state. Let us be thankful that we are not in their shoes and along with them let us pray for the compassion of the others, those safe from the dirt and the fall who hold in their hands the means of rescue.

Tomasito brought food for the statues, studied them, mimicked them, compared their measurements with those of Celeste and wondered at the differences life traces on the bodies of women. Thanks to his stares Cristina and the Friend got used to being naked and when the wind blew them off the pedestal, they were all ready to flex their muscles, crouch like scared rabbits and flee in terror while trying to dodge the sudden tempest bringing filth pouring down on their heads.

Some of the hostages, entwined in amorous embraces, did not manage to escape, and their destiny was cut short; others who suffered varying degrees of insomnia believed that all this was at last a dream and let themselves be carried away by the avalanche, eyes closed, delighted by the darkness. The draftees, so concerned about the mail, tried unsuccessfully to save from destruction the thousands of postage stamps they had accumulated in order to keep in touch with their sweethearts. Fragments of the London Times, clippings of visits of rock and roll groups to the Caribbean, photographs of the Pope, winter underwear, amazing bras in all colors, whips, chains, belts, maps, toptop secret documents, bones that had been gnawed by invisible animals floated among pieces of painted cardboard. The Caribbean and Europe turned into an ever growing conglomerated mass that not even the Arab kidnappers were able to put together again.

Perhaps it was the flimsiness of the mosquito net.

Perhaps it was the nondegradable fragrance of two hundred virgin vaginas.

The fact of the matter is that the leprosarium remained intact.

Cristina arrived all out of breath, the Friend close behind, trying not to lose sight of a single gesture, doing a great job of perfect spy to assure a future that in her mind would pay off handsomely in return for the costly betrayals that she thought only a select few were capable of. The surviving dictators pushed and shoved without being able to form a line, stepping on each other's heels, looking for someone to bribe, waiting for some down-and-outer who could be swindled by tales of power. They stampeded and elbowed each other, then suddenly finding themselves face to face with an old ally began to go through the proper motions:

—Good morning, good evening.
—Come have a drink and let's talk about the subversion of values a matter of common concern.
—Bring a map and a notebook to the General, clothes for Madame, prisoners both male and female for the police chiefs, lies for the press.
—Presents, presents.
—Let's initial our agreements.
—Let's get engaged, exchange rings.

But they soon realized that this was going nowhere and once again fell back into anonymity, noticed the filthy mud covering them head to foot and tried to breach the leprosarium, to get through the mosquito net that now had lost its consistency of tulle and had closed up like an enormous iron barrier before their very eyes.

LAMENTATIONS

Tomasito is crying. He beseeches one of the leper women then runs after another.

—I am a boy and I have to command. Let's get organized: this group here and this other one there; the heads of state to do forced labor; the draftees take care of national defense; we will build mansions

let's have a chew of tobacco
all together let's count up the tasks to be performed by our underlings

Tomasito is crying. Tomasito beseeches one of the leper women then runs after another, trying to caress them; then he turns mean and brandishes his youth; makes speeches about the future; points out that the world is collapsing around them; shows his apocalyptic finger, hides in order to pick his nose. Tomasito shits in variegated colors, remembers evenings with Celeste; resumes his siege of the virgins, shows them diagrams; shows some concern about his future.

Cristina looks around and sighs. From inside, the mosquito net looks white, almost like a cloud. The noise of the cave-in gives her goose pimples but she feels at ease with the Friend, especially now that she has quit talking and huddled into a ball is trying to hide the stack of notebooks filled with secret information that she has accumulated during her assignment with Cristina.

The air smells of damp earth, of spilled chocolate, and from time to time, Cristina recognizes some of the old places brought back by gusts of wind, but it is a memory without names, single details that cannot be put back together to describe to the Friend. And now she would so much like to. She longs to lose herself in those conversations again. Cristina searches for the Friend and tries to think of something that will arouse her attention and interest once again but the Friend had fled by then, hidden her things, and on the sly, is trying to ingratiate herself with Tomasito in order to continue her ascent.

The Friend is a miracle of information.

The Friend bounces up and down, boomerang. She is looking for a good observation post. She stations herself in the highest part of the mosquito net like a spider. Hand over hand to the top she scrutinizes the situation and takes notes. With unshakeable faith in the future of her area of expertise, she delves into the customs of the world stirring below and when she feels hungry, gnaws on her own feet.

The deposed heads of state bring a memorandum for the virgins. They knock on the surface of the mosquito net, promise great concessions. They have even written down the numbers of various Swiss bank accounts, a couple have enclosed written confessions of crimes that they never before admitted had taken place. They are in a tough spot. The cave-in has begun to bring down with it fresh corpses and the grimacing expressions of the tortured at being buried a second time by the avalanche seemed directed at their executioners.

But don't think that this time is without its opportunities for getting ahead. If we know anything it is that the chance to collect, assemble, and sell exists in every situation for those who know how to take advantage of it. Risking their place in line in front of the mosquito net some peddlers gather up buttons, scraps of tweed, plastic glasses for serving piña coladas; many of the collectors are carried away by the earthslide and their objects crumble into pieces so the collectors themselves become delectable treasure when some confused and overly ambitious competitor takes their shoes for merchandise. As in every mining endeavor there were countless victims; the horror of their appearance caused a rise in prices in a jittery market, regulated only by fear and envy.

The SELF MADE WOMAN emerges from the crowd. Even she is fighting for little shards of trinkets; even she tries to get ahead. She has more will than the others. She has more luck. When she was surprised by the avalanche, she happened to be carrying an empty potato sack. With a place to keep her booty she has an advantage.

> —She had an advantage.
> —She cheated.

Let's be frank. Let's not fool ourselves. Let's be honest. How did she get ahead? How did she gain that wealth admired and recognized by all? What methods did she use and what strategies?

With her elbows, like everybody else. Only her aim was better. Without any compassion. She wore blinders so that nothing would distract her. The SELF MADE WOMAN earns our admiration. Now she is idolized. Some reporters forget about the fight for survival and ask her for interviews.

> —What do you think of the era of Cristina?
> —Where did you study?
> —This technique of the fatal elbow thrust, is that something inborn?

A shame that there are no photos because she is really an inspiration for millions and millions of small entrepreneurs; her replies are brief; she is not interested in the press nor does the adulation butter her up. Her attention does not waver; she keeps fighting boldly for her wares and I assure you that she would have accumulated a king's ransom except for the limitations on how much her bag would hold.

The men secretly try to imitate her but by now it is too late. The other women don't understand that her triumph is not the result of good grooming. They do not share the fierce energy of her spirit. That's why in the night of the disaster the SELF MADE WOMAN shines like a glowworm.

LOVE AND DIPLOMACY

To our most hightly esteemed and admired leper women:

We hereby turn to you to request your aid in helping us to escape from our predicament of solitude and premature aging. We are surrounded by cardboard countries that are collapsing and threatening to carry us along in the ensuing havoc. We will put down all our weapons; we offer our slave labor to you unconditionally. We will turn the leprosarium into a garden, a palace, a government building, a kindergarten. Whatever duties you require of us will be carried out promptly. A psst, a wrinkle of the nose, a faint purse of the lips will suffice so that each one of us, constantly in a state of high alert, will comply instantly with your slightest whims. If there is any other requirement, any other desire that we have not anticipated that might be a condition for our acceptance into this most desired leprosarium, we will be more than eager to comply.

Awaiting your reply and the devoutly hoped for opening of the door we bid you farewell with   LOVE   RESPECT   OBEDIENCE   LONG LIVE THE FAMILY LONG LIVE THE LEPROSARIUM ETERNAL GLORY TO ITS OCCUPANTS

From all the rest of us, those on the outside

The letter took only a few minutes to write. The Friend saw everything from her sentry post and licked her fur and sharpened her claws to make ready for her future work with the SELF MADE WOMAN.

Tomasito and Cristina, hand in hand, walked up and down constantly inside the leprosarium. They congratulated themselves for being there. They recited to each other the tales of their own fate. Cristina, dressed in what was left of a tweed jacket and a Hawaiian skirt that she had luckily saved from the wreckage, stretched her legs and from time to time tried a dance step whose complete choreography would be possible only with the passage of time, when her body reached the lightness of a butterfly.

Tomasito and Cristina heard the clamor going on outside the mosquito net and were the first to notice the dirty piece of paper that the supplicants slipped under the fence.

—What shall we do?
—To whom shall we give it?
—They write as though the leper women could read it.
—They think the leper women are in charge of everything.
—They imagine that this is like one of those countries they left behind.
—They don't know that the mosquito net is just a promenade
    an amusement park with no games
    a movie theatre with no popcorn
    a silent film with sound

—Let's open the door so they can see for themselves.
—Let's let them come in and they will feel like ants when they hear the sound the leper women make with their knitting.
—No, let's leave them in the dark.
—Let's assure them that we are in charge of everything, queen and young deputy.
—To give some weight to our words let's demand that they surrender to us immediately all objects of value that they possess, all memory of better times still in their minds, all they know about flight.
—That is, this is to be a country club prison, without gates because the cave-in is sufficiently dangerous to keep anyone from trying to escape.

Tomasito's chest swelled with pride at the news of his power and an erection without any sentimental feelings attached prevented him from concentrating on the details of his future government.

MY COUNTRY, FORWARD! MY LITTLE DUMMIES   MY BELOVED INTERNA-TIONAL DIGNITARIES   FORWARD   FORWARD   HERE WE WILL BE SAFE HERE YOU WILL LIVE BY PAYING FAIR TAXES   MY DEAR VERY DEAR FRIENDS   COLLEAGUES   JOURNALISTS   FORWARD TO SAVE YOURSELVES FROM THE END I WILL GUIDE YOU MY DEPUTY HAS THE MAP   SILENCE SILENCE   SILENCE   SILENCE   LISTEN NOW TO THE ANTHEM OF THIS LEPROSARIUM

Cristina once again felt she was back in the circus of her past life. The group of survivors allowed her to picture Francisco's pleasures. For the first time she sensed the convolutions of the soul of the man who had been her companion, why he fought his enemies with such ferocity, and above all, how her own presence had evoked for him the pride she felt now standing in full view, her straightbacked little deputy Tomasito by her side.

—Tomasito, walk a few steps behind me.

—Yes, my queen.

—Tomasito, organize your own police force so that nobody can compete with our power.

—Tomasito, don't cheat on me. One of your duties will be to practice masturbation like all powerful leaders, since they cannot trust anybody if they want to get a good night's sleep. Tomasito, make love to yourself every day during the siesta for there is no greater happiness than knowing that one is totally self-sufficient. The economy of the leprosarium will be like this love that we have for ourselves. It will need nobody, but will feed on itself forever.

So Tomasito and Cristina talked on and on, speaking to each other in a formal manner, bowing, trying out the routines of terror and submission. But when the doors of the leprosarium were opened, the throng showed no interest in staying put. Nobody lingered to hear the speech. Nobody noticed Tomasito standing beside Cristina in the pose of national hero. They just didn't care.

My dears:
The truth is they shit on him.

What happened was that the SELF MADE WOMAN had made a statistical study of the approximate chances of getting into the leprosarium, and once she got the results, everybody knew they would get in sooner or later. As far as skinny Cristina and Tomasito were concerned, nobody even saw them. Covered with dirt, stones and scratches, starving after the long wait, the only thing that mattered was to fling themselves onto the grass, flowers, greens and to eat, devour everything they could put their hands on.

When they all collapsed on the ground exhausted, to fall into a fitful sleep disturbed by nightmares of the past and the future, the Friend came down from her post and lay down beside the SELF MADE WOMAN who was sleeping peacefully, her bag held firmly between her legs and her tailored suit impeccable. The Friend examined her in detail, tried to eavesdrop on her dreams, snatched from her ears fragments of unfinished conversations, removed bits of dirt from her feet so that she could absorb her intimate odors and weaknesses. She wrote everything down carefully in her notebook and waited, eyes wide open, for the dawn of a new day and another marvelous friendship.

THE SONG OF
THE LEPER WOMEN

Back and forth they went knitting during the night, walking over the sleeping bodies. In unison they would bend down to capture a caterpillar and gulp it down with pleasure. Fat ones. Soft ones. What a touching song. The sleeping crowd began to weep inconsolably. The leprosarium filled with water; the bodies of the sleeping floated gently on the salty rain so when morning came grass and flowers had sprouted anew. Once again there was food, once again the leprosarium was a paradise within the confines of the mosquito net which had recovered its texture of tulle.

It was a great era. The Friend was the only one who did not graze or sleep, intent on the slightest gesture of the SELF MADE WOMAN. But the SELF MADE WOMAN was completely happy in her spiritual retreat, as she described the new circumstances to herself. She had never breathed so freely, not even in the many spas she used to visit when she was exhausted by work and needed to be recharged with energy to keep conquering new positions, each one higher than the last, in multinational organizations. No, she was very satisfied.

The Friend was forced to conclude that without discontent, there was no way for her to establish a relationship, construct an intimacy that would render her contact vulnerable. In that world, the virgins had turned them all into a loveable herd. Every night, their song saddened and softened the souls so that the bodies could nourish themselves throughout the day with the left-overs of the deepest nostalgia.

—I seem to hear a bolero in there.

—No, it must be one of those tangos that were so popular in the fifties.

—Could it be a radio?

—Shhh. I don't want them to hear us before we are absolutely certain that we can save them.

—If we hadn't been able to stop this cave-in, these guys would have ended up buried.

—In what language are they singing?

—What strange accompaniment.

—There's a smell sort of like water.

—Shhh.

It was an international rescue force organized by the Association of Friends of Order. The lead team had noticed earth tremors, one of its members had fallen down an elevator shaft that seemed to keep going to the center of the earth. His final wail remained engraved on the memory of all those attending the meeting who swore to investigate the incident. The similarity between that event and the countless other occasions when people and objects disappeared down holes opened overnight meant archeologists, paleontologists and seismologists were all included in the expedition.

The one who was really on the ball, however, was a speculator in real estate. He attended a meeting of researchers in Stockholm, a panel discussion in Beirut, the election of new delegates in Cartagena, as well as countless functions organized to collect funds. His conclusion was crystal clear: "What is needed is a strong hand." In his mind, accustomed as he was to overseeing the conversion of miserable rooming houses into luxury condos for busy professional couples in competition with people like him, the strategy was as plain as day. They would have to find a profit motive, and once that was found, nothing would be able to stem the flood of inventions, suggestions, and sure things put forward by people all fired up by the possibility of getting ahead.

And so a publicity campaign was organized that covered the four corners of the globe. A frenzy of finding lost objects ensued. Everybody walked around with their eyes glued to the ground. Buttons turned up, addresses of dentists recommended by a toothless aunt, telephone numbers of frustrated lovers at subway exits, needles, rings, the screw that made the enormous locomotive go that had stood idle for twenty years; things that helped clear up mysteries now of no interest to anyone, keys, oh how many keys and handkerchiefs and dried snot and even a feather of a pre-hispanic animal. Finally, the woman who cleaned Father Gabriel's church got in touch with the real estate tycoon.

—I will take you, I will track him to hell itself if necessary. Who does he think he is anyway the cute little priest, leaving without saying a word. He may even have a mistress and everything. I am convinced that everything is trembling and falling to pieces because of his sins. I am sure of it; ever since the day of the MELTING of our beloved Teitelbaum; since that day I have not closed my eyes one minute and now I know where he has gone; slippery old man, what is he up to. The earth itself is indignant. Here we don't need any rescue. PUNISHMENT. PUNISHMENT. THAT IS WHAT WE NEED.

It goes without saying that the world divided between those who demanded punishment for the lack of moral fiber that had confounded them and the compassionate and curious, of different ideological stripes, who dreamed about reading a meticulous report, composed in democratic fashion by all the eye witnesses, following consultation with prudent scientists who would vouch for the results.

The real estate tycoon was delighted by these discussions because now nobody remembered that he had promised huge prizes for the first ones to get an operation going. The team milling around at the moment in front of the mosquito net had been chosen after the most careful deliberations subject to the approving eye of the sponsoring tycoon. The numerous finds had made the group feel very optimistic. They felt confident in the future and the moment they picked up their ears to identify the song of the leper women, nobody remembered that they had signed away the rights to any lands that might be discovered, a requirement of their patron and generous billionaire. Only the music interested them and the pristine damp air that came out in whiffs from the leprosarium.

RE-ENCOUNTERS

173

Because they had organized the expedition in order to find something new and in order to solve an old problem. Perhaps because they had read too much about the brilliant void experienced by astronauts in interplanetary flights. Perhaps because many of them were too young or too old and believed fervently in the need for a completely fresh experience, perhaps for all these reasons, they all felt suddenly saddened when the traveling salesman, who had the job of cataloging all unknown objects found during the trip, ran across an address book undoubtedly dropped during a moment of crisis and recognized it as belonging to his daughter.

—So then it was true.
—People lived here.
—The locks.
—Bikinis.

—Everything they had was identical to ours, only a little more up-to-date, as if they had been bought last year.

—They must have been rich.
—Right about here they must have escaped, after all the avalanche had already stopped.

The traveling salesman rubbed his hands, his eyes, his soul. For years and years, day and night, he had crisscrossed the world searching for his little daughter who ran away one day when he asked her to go with him to pick out the pair of sunglasses that would make him look most distinguished. In a matter of seconds she disappeared into thin air. It did no good for him to keep trying on pair after pair of sunglasses, she never returned, and now, this address book in her very own handwriting, still with the round letters she made when she was twelve years old, plunged him into a feverish hope that he might see her again.

—EDELMIRA! EDELMIRITA! It's your papa come to find you, to give you chocolates. Edelmira, Edelmirita . . .

The SELF MADE WOMAN was sleeping on the far side of the mosquito net and didn't hear the shouts of her father. The Friend, keeping a vigil at her side, smelled an opportunity and whispered into her ear: Edelmira, Edelmirita . . . If she was Edelmira their friendship would know no bounds, she would be the first, the only person to know her real name, the only one with access to the story of before the triumph, occasion for secrets, bribes, blackmail.

Creeping crawling scheming spider, the so charming Friend comes close too close to the daughter of the traveling salesman. He shouts and she murmurs; between the one and the other they bring on the SELF MADE WOMAN's dreadful nightmare of abandonment. She turns over in her dream, kicks and zap! breaks the Friend's neck with the fury of one of her famous elbow thrusts.

The SELF MADE WOMAN was totally efficient, even in her dreams she could rid herself of the danger of being manipulated. Nobody knew about the Friend's death. She floated for eight hours on the river of tears and later was absorbed by the earth and then turned into a sharp blade of yellow grass that even the caterpillars refused to creep over.

When the traveling salesman entered the mosquito net he immediately recognized his daughter's face but when she opened her eyes and looked at him with such a genuine lack of recognition, he knew it would take him several lifetimes to make her return to the shop where they had seen each other for the last time. By a stroke of luck he had brought with him the sunglasses he bought on that occasion, and murmuring "excuse me miss" he mingled with the rest of the inhabitants of the leprosarium who noticed nothing strange because they were grazing with the patience and lethargy of people who have just awakened.

For Rodrigo de León the rejection of Tomasito was harder to take. He had to endure a long tirade about the shame of living with a father who smelled of fish and was forever tightening the screws to make sure that his son would prove himself a real little man. What does it matter, what does it matter now that I am a deputy. See you never. See you never. What do I care about that baby Celeste. I cooked up a romance with her just to prove my manliness. I never was interested in her curls. I never liked her plans; I was full up to here with the magazines she showed me and the shirts she made for me in sewing class. Enough of that hell. My future is here.

Touched by the hatred that Tomasito expressed for Celeste, Rodrigo de León told him that he had ordered her elimination. At that Tomasito flew into such a fury and kicked him in the knees so hard that Father Gabriel and the cleaning woman, now overjoyed at having tracked down her old client, had to take turns carrying Rodrigo de León on their backs.

What rejoicing when Cristina caught sight of Father Gabriel. Now so thin, she had completely forgotten about her problems with the church in the era of low-cut necklines and the rumors about the Father's involvement in the conspiracy concerning the jew Teitelbaum. She only saw a tiny little emaciated figure, almost her own size. It took them a short time, only two or three hours, to bring each other up to date, to complain about the cold in their benumbed birdbone bodies and it was a good thing that they didn't have much more to say to one another because a sudden gust of wind blew through the open door of the mosquito net, wafted them aloft and sent them flying off into the distance, through the tunnels of the crumbled exile.

THE RETURN

The rescue team attached each one to a separate cord and now lead them away, content after grazing, delivered of sadness after all those tears. So many are returning. The deposed heads of state. The homesick draftees. Rodrigo de León wounded. Tomasito unwillingly. The two hundred virgins tied into an enormous gray package, their heads outside breathing in unison. They return now expecting nothing. When they are lifted through the hole they will rub their eyes   even if it's cloudy, this light is different. This light is disturbing. This light. This fucking light.